Lewis Warsh writes poetry, fiction and autobiography. As a publisher, he has been steadfast in his dedication to works of distinguished artistic vision, keeping the books he publishes alive with a grace and spirit perhaps typified by the name of his press, United Artists. Lewis Warsh lives in Brooklyn.

OTHER BOOKS BY LEWIS WARSH

Poetry

The Suicide Rates (1967)
Highjacking (1968)
Moving Through Air (1968)
Chicago (1969)
Dreaming As One (1971)
Long Distance (1971)
Immediate Surrounding (1974)
Today (1974)
Blue Heaven (1977)
Hives (1978)
Methods of Birth Control (1983)
The Corset (1986)
Information from the Surface of Venus (1987)
Avenue of Escape (1995)
Private Agenda (1996)

Fiction

Agnes & Sally (1984)
A Free Man (1991)

Autobiography

Part of My History (1972)
The Maharajah's Son (1978)
Bustin's Island '68 (1996)

Translation

Night of Loveless Nights by Robert Desnos (1973)

MONEY UNDER THE TABLE

by

Lewis Warsh

Some of these stories first appeared in *Lingo, Long News, Pequod* and in the anthology *2000andWhat?* Thanks to the editors: Michael Gizzi, Barbara Henning, Mark Rudman, Karl Roeseler and David Gilbert. Special thanks to Allegra David, Gary Sullivan, Bill Kushner and Wang Ping.

Cover photograph of Lewis Warsh by Marie Warsh
All other photographs by Howard Gelman
Cover and book design by Clare Rhinelander

Printed by McNaughton & Gunn on acid-free paper
Printed in the United States of America

The names, characters and events portrayed in these pages are the product of the author's imagination. Any resemblance to actual persons, living or dead, or to real events is entirely coincidental.

© 1996 and 1997 by Lewis Warsh

All rights reserved. Duplication or reproduction by any mechanical or electronic means is strictly prohibited, except for brief quotation by a reviewer, critic or friend.

ISBN 0-9639192-3-7
First Edition. 1997

Trip Street Press Books are distributed by:
Small Press Distribution
1814 San Pablo Avenue
Berkeley, CA 94702
1/800-869-7553 or 510/549-3336

Trip Street Press • P. O. Box 190201 • San Francisco, CA 94119 USA

MONEY UNDER
THE TABLE

for George & Chris Tysh

CONTENTS

Love is harder to give up than life.

— *Celine*

CRACK

He handed me his card as we stood in the hallway. We were waiting for the elevator, side by side, our shoulders touching, and he reached into his pocket for his wallet and fished out his card. It had his name on it, in gold letters, his address and phone number. If I ever needed help, he said, I shouldn't hesitate to call. I assumed he thought I needed help (if not now, then someday), though I didn't know how he could tell. I had been alert and restless all day but after the encounter with the stranger in the hallway I began looking forward to going home, getting into bed with a long novel, and falling asleep for twelve hours. The elevator was crowded; I stepped in and turned a full circle so I was facing the door. For a moment the smell of perfume, the physical contact with people I knew only by sight, the swift plunge from the fortieth to the twentieth floor, made me feel like I was going to faint. One woman, who I saw almost every day as I passed through the marble lobby, was pressing against me from behind, her hand on my thigh. But when I turned to say something she didn't even smile.

The phone rang that night and Irina answered it and said it was for me. The curtains were billowing at the open window and the radio was playing a song by Nat King Cole, Irina's favorite singer. The song matched my mood (sullen, restless: why couldn't I sleep?), and the temperature outside had dropped ten degrees in the last hour.

I was wearing the same pin-striped shirt I had worn that afternoon when I met the man in the hallway, the man with the card (which was in my jacket pocket), but I had removed my tie. I stared through the window, parting the curtains with one hand and lifting the phone to my ear. The woman who lived in the apartment above us was walking her dog at the edge of the curb. I tried to visualize the face of the man in the hallway but all I could remember was the bandaid on his chin where he had cut himself shaving.

"It's for me" I said to Irina when the phone rang again. She folded the newspaper she was reading and left the room. By now, there was another song on the radio and the voice on the phone said "Remember me? I gave you my card." I wanted to ask him how he got my number since it was he who had given me his, not the other way around. I don't have a card and even if I did I'm not one for giving my number away to strangers, even those who attract me. I knew that Irina was listening to the conversation at the door of the living room. Or beyond the door where I couldn't see her, but only a shadow. The voice on the phone apologized for calling once and hanging up. "A bad connection," he said, but I knew there was some other reason. I knew that when I got off the phone I would have to tell Irina who called and what had been said. It was our habit, after five years of marriage, to report back to one another about everything that happened when we were apart. And since we're apart most of the time there's always a lot to say.

She was standing in the hallway, in the vestibule near the mailboxes, when I returned home from work. I had loosened my tie on the subway ride home and I was carrying my jacket over my arm. The day was late spring and evening had slipped by without the usual drop in temperature. As I tried to brush by her, I had never seen her before, she put her hand on my arm and asked me if I would give her ten dollars. Not loan, give. Even when she asked me for the money, I noticed, she didn't look at me directly. Didn't make eye contact the way people do when they meet for the first time. When you want something from someone you look them in the eye (that's what I do). I knew I had a twenty in my wallet, a five and some ones. It was a warm evening in late spring and I had stayed at work longer than usual. I had no idea how long she was waiting in the lobby, or if she was waiting for me.

I asked the man on the phone where he got my number and he said "Bob" and I said "Bob who?" but it was just a technicality like running outside the baseline. I knew a lot of Bobs, from childhood on: Bobby Kennedy, Bobby McGee. I was glad that he had called but I didn't say that. Some music, the ideal form of communication (no words), filled my head, but I didn't say that either. I knew, if I said anything, Irina (who was listening) would ask: "What did you mean?" Later that night, lying in bed, she would question me about what he wanted and I would say: I don't even know him, I never saw him until this afternoon when I was leaving work. Then Irina would roll on top of me and let her nightgown slip over her shoulders. She has a closet filled with nightgowns, some of which she's never worn, at least not for me. This one was yellow, my favorite color, with doves embroidered on the sleeves.

That night, as I was going through the pockets of my jacket, I found the card which the stranger had given me. Irina was already in bed reading a volume of Proust. Before getting into bed she usually puts on lipstick: *mango, blushing tulip, panic pink.* Then she reads to me or we listen to music before going to sleep. She was lying in bed reading with the book balanced on her knees. Her knees (raised) made a tent of the sheets and blankets. Soon, I thought, we would no longer need the covers which had kept us warm that winter. We could sleep in the nude, with the window open, like we did last summer, and the summer before.

The woman in the hallway told me she could get me anything I wanted. "Anything" (I felt sleepy). She held the bill I had given her in her hand, not anxious to leave, no longer desperate for whatever she had needed that had inspired her to ask me for money. Now that she had the money she could get what she needed whenever she wanted. She had stringy brown shoulder-length hair and wore an old winter coat with wooden buttons. Possibly she didn't want to feel that she was just taking from me without giving, without at least offering me something in return. The word "anything" hung in the air between us like a falling leaf buffeted by the wind.

The next day at work a woman named Sara asked me if I would join her for lunch. We sat at a table near a window in a French restaurant and she touched my knee. She put her hand on my upper thigh under the table and told me she knew I was married but... "I can't help myself," she said. She was biting her lips and crying and I asked the waiter to bring her an aspirin but she shook her head and dabbed at her eyes, the eyeliner running down her cheeks. People at nearby tables began poking one another and staring at me angrily as if I were the cause of her suffering. I looked through the window of the restaurant and noticed that the people on the street were wearing less clothing than the day before. The light on the street was golden and the buds were soaking up the sun.

I felt like I was part of everyone I knew. I felt I was divided into parts and that I wasn't a person who could say "I did this" and really mean that it was "me." The "me" seemed like someone else, or everyone else, and not only that: not only did I have to keep the faces of everyone I knew suspended in my mind at all times, but I also had to keep track of the lights of the city, the cars, and even the music floating out at me from an open window. I felt I was a composite of all these things; the absence of any one thing was the source of my sadness, my regret. If you asked about "me" I would say: look at the light on the side of this building. Look at this tree.

When I arrived home Irina said "He called again" and I thought of Sara. That night, lying in bed with Irina, I had to admit that I was thinking about Sara, how she had wept in the restaurant. It was a hopeless feeling to make love to one person and think of another. The man with the card asked (when I told him about this): "Does it happen often?" The next day when I saw Sara at work I blushed but she averted her eyes (too painful). The man with the card said he had his office down the hall from mine and when I stepped inside he locked the door behind him and loosened his tie.

The advantage of friendship is that there's no jealousy involved. Plato said that, I think, in the *Phaedrus*, which I read in college. "To be curious about that which is not my concern, while I am still in ignorance of my own self, would be ridiculous" (Plato said). He said: "In the friendship of the lover there is no real kindness" (of course not). The man with the card said, we were in his office, "Why don't you make yourself comfortable?" I thought of the time my mother, who left me with a babysitter when I was a child so she could go back to work, came home early one day, dropped her raccoon coat onto the living room rug, and announced: I'm quitting.

She was wearing the same coat and dress she had been wearing the week before. And this time, when I gave her the money and she said "anything," I followed. Across the street, down an alley, into the basement of a tenement. This is it, I said to myself, this is what I want, always want. She reached behind her and took my hand and lead me into the darkness of rats scurrying and black plastic garbage bags and cans. It was the engine of the building down here, all the cables and meters. I couldn't imagine going any deeper but I still wasn't sinking. My head was above water and I knew a few nouns and adjectives so that describing it to myself was still an endeavor I could aspire to at a later date. I heard voices (do rats speak?) and someone asked: "Who's that?" Someone was standing guard, in the darkness, like a sentry. And then the woman said, simply: "It's me, I brought a friend."

We were on our knees on the floor of the basement amid the garbage cans and rats. The vial of white powder had fallen from her hands and I lit a match but we couldn't find it. The woman and the men behind us were cursing and someone was laughing. It was probably odd for them to see a man with a jacket and tie crawling around on his knees. Until this happened I have to admit I didn't know it was what I needed. I saw Irina, just a flash, but she wasn't in bed reading. I could see her body floating out the window above the city. Irina, in her red nightgown, an adjective, a clause, her arms outstretched above the rooftops. It was all I could do to prevent myself from following her, but I knew that the experience of flying would be different for me. I knew if I stepped off the ledge I would plunge like a rocket to the pavement.

When I came into work the next day there was a vase and a single red rose on my desk. Sara beamed at me from across the office and I realized it was her doing. I thought of what I could do to reciprocate, a rose for a rose, amazed that she didn't hate me after what had happened the day before. She leaned over my desk and pushed her breasts against my shoulder and I felt a twinge in my neck as if I'd slept under an open window. Later, I said to her, I have to go out for awhile: take a message if anyone calls. And she nodded, subservient, no questions asked: I'll do what you want.

I put my hand through the broken window but I didn't feel anything. "It's like having an orgasm, isn't it?" the woman said, wiping away the blood. She had taken off her blouse but I didn't notice as she gave herself a sponge bath with the water from a basement tap. I no longer knew what "feeling" meant, only "intensity" seemed to convey the sensations I had previously described as "love" or "anger." The excitement was no longer prearranged but seemed to blur my sense of what was most familiar. It was like my first night in Paris, after taking the boat-train from London. Or Venice, getting lost in the maze of alleyways, canals and streets. So when I came to a new feeling I had to stop for a moment, like a tourist, and say: this is it.

I sat at my desk at work, in the large open area where everyone can spy on everyone else, and leafed through a book of photographs of Marilyn Monroe. I had a hard time focusing on words but I could still look at pictures and I kept going back to the one where she's running from the ocean in a white bathing suit holding an umbrella with red dots. "Obviously posed" I kept saying to myself, and then "larger than life." I was tempted (who knew who was watching me?) to press my lips to the different parts of her body when the phone rang and it was Sara to say she was feeling under the weather (her phrase) and wasn't coming in. There was a pause and she said "I'll be expecting you" and then "don't worry, you won't catch anything." Her assumption that I was planning to visit her caught me off guard and I started stuttering. "I'm b-b-backed up here," I said, which wasn't true. There's never enough work to do — I spend most of my day reading the newspaper — and she knew it.

The man who gave me the card locked the door of his office behind him. There was someone else in the room but he didn't introduce us. Instead, he addressed the stranger, a young man in a suit and tie. He said: "Ernie, I think our friend here needs a wake-up call. Don't you?" I was standing in the center of the room with my feet planted firmly on the carpet. Ernie walked out from around the desk, stood in front of me, and punched me in the stomach. I fell to my knees and he hit me in the back of the neck and kicked me in the ribs as if I were a dog. "That's enough," the man with the card said. He knelt beside me and turned me over onto my back and slapped my face lightly with his fingers. I felt his hands on me, loosening the knot of my tie and unbuttoning my pants, and I felt like reaching out and pushing him away but I didn't have the strength. "I told you to call me," he said. "This is something to remember me by." He snapped his fingers. Ernie disappeared for a minute and returned with a glass of water. He propped my head beneath his arm and tilted the glass to my lips but the water spilled out of the corners of my mouth and down my chin. I tried to stand up but he kept pushing me back against the carpet. The office was empty except for a desk and a chair. There were no diplomas on the wall to indicate that he was a doctor or a broker. "Now you know what it feels like when you hurt someone," he said. "Like a punch in the stomach."

That evening, when I told Irina I was going out, she retaliated by saying that her ex-husband Sid was in town and they were meeting for a drink. In the past, I always expressed anger when she told me she was meeting Sid. He came to New York maybe twice a year and called her up every time. But this time it meant nothing to me. I genuinely hoped they had fun together. I thought of all my old lovers and how happy I would feel if they called me up. Then Irina said: "A woman named Sara called" and I stopped what I was doing. She said: "You're going to meet her, aren't you?" and ran into the kitchen in tears. I guess she assumed I was being unfaithful to her with the woman from my office and I realized that if she thinks that she doesn't know me at all. I had never lied to her once in the five years we were together. If I was going to see Sara I wouldn't try to hide it. "Believe me," I said, putting my hands on her shoulders, "I'm just going for a walk," but she wasn't listening.

This time I went directly across the street to the basement. I lit matches to see my way through the dark. "I knew you were coming," the woman said when she saw me. Some of the faces of the people there were already familiar to me but none of them said hello. There were two people making love on a mattress in a corner with the woman on top. I took out my wallet and emptied it on the floor of the basement. "You must have robbed a bank," the woman said when she saw all the tens and twenties. "It's Cash

McCall," one of the men in the background said, and everyone laughed. The woman scooped up the money and said "I'll be right back." I leaned back against a garbage can and lit a cigarette, trying to blend in.

My father was a dentist and encouraged me to follow in his profession but I dropped out of dental school in my first semester: it just wasn't for me. After that, I took some art courses, painting and sculpture, and for a few years I lived in a loft and attended parties and openings and even had a show, but nothing sold. I was going to have a second show but the gallery folded and I began doing office work, first as a temp, then as a fulltimer so I could get the benefits. For awhile I continued painting after work and then I met Irina and we moved to the apartment uptown and the past began to fade. All my old paintings are still in storage somewhere. Occasionally I get an invitation from an old friend who's having a show but I never attend. The office work involves pieces of paper (non-threatening) and voices on the phone. And then there are my co-workers, Sara and the others, with whom I try to get along, if only to make the job more interesting. It's hard to spend forty hours a week with the same people and not feel intimate in some way. I would have to be blind not to realize that Sara was falling in love with me, but I didn't want to admit it for fear I would do something to hurt her. I became the personification of indifference: who cares what you feel? She leaned over my desk and I felt myself slipping down the side of a well. I felt like I was lost in an endless sentence, a maze of words, where my only escape was to reach out and touch her breasts: what was being offered. We would go to lunch and she would ask me about my past and I would tell her: "My father was a dentist..." but I knew she wasn't listening. I could feel the tip of her shoe against my leg and her head would tilt to one side but I kept on talking if only to appease the guilt, the mixture of guilt and longing. At night, I would lie in bed and Irina would read to me from the volume of Proust which she was finishing, and I felt like I was sinking, clause after clause, into the maze of words, where the only escape was to roll over on top of her and lift her nightgown over her breasts, the pale blue nightgown or the silk one, the one she had worn with her ex-husband. I deluded myself into thinking that thoughts were a form of action and that it was permissible to think about Sara while I was making love to Irina. I couldn't understand why Irina, with whom I had lived for five years, was incapable of reading my mind. It made me self-conscious, as if someone were looking over my shoulder as I turned the pages of a magazine with pictures of naked women in poses that invited you to enter their bodies. I could even pretend for a moment that these women weren't being abused, fucked-over, that most of them hated men. By day, during the week, I would try to avoid Sara's advances. I would discourage her, I would literally push her away when she leaned over my desk, while at night I would pretend I was lifting her dress, right in the office, when everyone else had gone home. We would go to lunch together, maybe twice a week, at a small French restaurant near Eighth Avenue which we thought of as "our place." The same waiter led us to the same table and chatted with Sara in French. I let her pretend that I was available, that something was happening between us. I even let her hold my hand as we waited for the food to arrive. But most of all I never stopped talking.

The woman in the basement said I could spend the night there if I wanted or I could go with her to an abandoned building on the Lower East Side where she sometimes slept. I unlaced my shoes and sat on the edge of the mattress and I could sense that she was dozing off, that she was going to sleep in her clothing. I pulled at her hair and said "wake up" and she started cursing at me so I stopped. By now I was used to the sound of the rats and the hum of machines. At that moment I felt I could make love to anyone, woman or man.

Everyone who lived in the basement had a name: Aloha, Conrad,

Vitamin G, Washout, Bedtime Story. "You can call me Sylvie," the woman said, after we spent our first night together. She apologized for falling asleep when I was most awake and promised that she would make it up to me somehow. She leaned over and bit me on the side of my neck and told me that she had been living in the basement for almost a year. And before that? I asked. There was a child, a husband, a house in the suburbs. There was a station wagon, with which she drove her son to school, trips to Europe every summer. As she told me her life story, she began licking a callous on the side of her thumb. She took my hand and placed it between her legs. I tried not to think what the man with the card had told me about what it felt like to experience pain, that it was worse than a punch in the stomach or a broken jaw. Is that what he said?

After a week in the basement I decided to return to my apartment, what I thought of as my "old apartment," and visit with Irina. I had lost my keys in the basement, the buzzer system wasn't working, so I waited in the vestibule until someone let me in. It was the woman who lived above us, walking her dog. I hadn't shaved in a week and I don't think she recognized me at first. Her dog was black with a white spot on the top of its head and began pawing the cuffs of my trousers, as if I had something he wanted. The woman, who was in her early forties, tugged at the leash and began climbing the stairs. Once, when I returned home from work, about a year ago, she had been sitting on the living room sofa next to Irina, who was showing her photographs from our album. She had stood up to leave almost immediately and lowered her eyes as she brushed by me. Her hair was almost down to her waist and as I followed her up the stairs I had to stop myself from touching it. At the third landing I paused to catch my breath but she continued on, without saying goodbye.

At first, when I knocked on the door of the apartment, no one answered. Then a man's voice said "Who is it?" and I shouted out my name. It was Sid, Irina's ex-husband. I could hear Irina's voice in the background: "Who is it?" All the furniture was gone and there was a stack of cartons against one wall and an open suitcase on the floor filled with Irina's clothing. "I don't think she wants to see you," Sid said. "She's moving out." Then Irina appeared and began pounding at my chest with her fists. "I think you better leave," Sid said. He took my arm and tried to steer me out the door but I pushed him away. "Five years," Irina shouted. "Five fucking years." I wanted to explain that I accepted the blame for what had gone wrong, that she shouldn't punish herself, that it had all been my fault. The apartment looked tiny with no furniture and I couldn't imagine how we had ever lived there for so long without killing one another. The fact that we had survived five years together in such a close space was a kind of triumph. I wondered what she had done with all my possessions, all the things we had bought together and which, in a sense, were half mine. Out on the landing, Sid pressed a fifty dollar bill into my palm. "If you're going to kill yourself," he said, "do it in style."

Sylvie disappeared for a few hours every afternoon. She had a friend who worked in a hotel in midtown who let her use a room. The rest of the time we sat on the mattress in the basement listening to the radio or playing cards. If the weather was especially warm, we went to Tompkins Square Park and sat on a bench. My money had run out and we lived on the money Sylvie made at the hotel. As soon as she arrived at the hotel she called a woman named Dora and Dora told her the day's schedule and what each of the customers said they wanted. One afternoon, when Sylvie was at work, I dozed off on the mattress in the basement and when I woke up Aloha was kneeling over me. She was an Egyptian woman, with graying hair, who always wore a long striped ankle-length gown. "I wanted to surprise you," she said. "Sylvie won't mind." She unbuckled my pants, lifted her dress, and climbed on top of me. She leaned forward so that her mouth was against my ear and began humming a song that sounded like "Some Enchanted Evening," but more uptempo, in the old bossa nova style Irina and I danced to when we first met. Afterwards, she fell asleep in my arms, which is how Sylvie found us when she returned from the hotel. I sat up, quickly, as if one of the overhead pipes had exploded in my head, thinking Sylvie would be angry at me, but she just laughed, as if to say: We all need our privacy, don't we? Then she took off her clothing and joined us, with Aloha in the middle. I remember, hours later, leaning back against the basement wall smoking a cigarette, watching them make love, something I'd never seen before except in pornographic movies. *Two women.* My head began aching with the thought of all the time I'd wasted in my life, all the possibilities I'd backed away from, fearful of the risk, that I might go crazy if I acted one way and not another, deluding myself into thinking that happiness was a function of order, that security was like a tunnel where you never look back. Even when I was painting pictures I was never *inside* the painting (an experience which the painters I admired most had described) but thinking of the final result, wanting it to be over with so I could play the role of spectator (which I preferred), admiring my work from a distance as if someone else had done it. All my old paintings, locked away somewhere, resembled coffins, dead objects, and the last thing I wanted was to create something for others to admire, as if they were speaking a eulogy over my grave. What I wanted was to be like one of the stripes on Aloha's gown, not a line on a map between two points but something that was somehow bent out of shape and restored to life at the same time, so that the act of healing would go on as long as the body kept moving, but with no contours. I was sitting on the edge of the mattress, leaning back against the wall having these thoughts, when Sylvie looked up from between Aloha's legs and said, reaching out and taking my hand: "Don't be sad, honey, we haven't forgotten you," and we all laughed.

THE MERIT SYSTEM

He assumed he was doing her a favor by telling her what he was feeling. He assumed that honesty in any form was a virtue and that there was no point in keeping secrets from the person you lived with, pretending you felt one way when the opposite was true. It was only later, when he left the apartment and walked across town to his brother's apartment to spend the night, that he began feeling guilty about hurting her feelings. He realized that the only reason he had said what he did was to get back at her for something equally hideous that she had said to him a few weeks before. He knew that he didn't want to go through life hurting people. What he had said to her, her reaction, the way he was feeling about it now, was familiar to him. He had played out this scenario years ago with other women. It never occurred to him that she might be relieved by what he had said, that she had sensed the depth of his enmity towards her for years (impossible to disguise when you live side by side), and that she was growing weary of living in the shadow of the illusion that they were going to spend the rest of their lives together. No, on the contrary, she wasn't suffering at all. The minute he walked out the door she put on her suede jacket and went downstairs to the bar across the street to be with her friends. "I shouldn't have spoken to her like that," he said to himself, replaying everything he had ever done in his life to hurt anyone. It's possible that she *was* suffering over what he had said, but she wasn't the type who was going to wallow in her unhappiness. Didn't he know that about her? She wasn't going to sit home alone and brood. If she was going to drink, which she did almost every night whether she was suffering or not, she would do it among friends. It proved how little he knew about her after ten years of living together to think that she was lying in bed at that moment suffering because of what he had said. That his words really had that kind of effect. He had spoken to her, he had told her what he was feeling, he had tried to be honest with her. There was no way what he was telling her couldn't be hurting her in some way. He assumed, after all their years together, that he had the power to hurt her. He didn't realize that in the course of their life together she had managed to insulate her real feelings for fear of getting hurt. The disguise she wore had become more comfortable, more fleece-like, than her own skin. After awhile she had forgotten what she had been trying to hide to begin with. It was only while he was telling her what he was feeling, that he had stopped loving her, that she remembered why she had armored herself in the first place. The look on her face, which he interpreted as a sign of suffering, was really the shock of remembering that this was the moment she had been preparing for, like the meaning of a moat around a castle isn't clear until the castle is attacked. Her expression was also an acknowledgment of the fact that she had known for years that he no longer loved her, so it was no big deal for her to be hearing it now. His actions, over the last few years, had communicated his lack of love for her, so that hearing it all now was a redundancy, to say the least, like he was trying to underline something that was already written in boldfaced letters, large enough even a blind person could read them. It was like he was trying to rub it in, making it worse by talking about it, and it was all she could do to prevent herself from yawning. "I just want to be completely honest with you," he repeated, and she nodded at him quickly, as if she understood everything, as if she agreed with him, as if she admired him for his truth-telling, as if she was about to get down on her knees and beg him to stay, as if she cared.

After he left, she brushed her blonde hair over her shoulders, staring at herself in the full-length mirror on the inside door of her closet. She had a sullen expression on her face, even when she smiled. She put on the suede jacket which she had recently stolen from A&S and walked to the restaurant-bar across the street. The bar was called Leon's. It was always crowded. Her best friend Kathy worked there as a waitress. Other friends hung out there as well and she sat in a corner booth talking to them all, smoking and occasionally yawning because the conversation was dragging. She would wait till the bar closed and she was alone with her friend before she told her, almost as a joke, what Tom had said to her that night. She would present it almost as an afterthought, as if talking about it wasn't important. She would describe how solemn he had been about it all. Her friend, the waitress, wore a tight black off-the-shoulder blouse and a short skirt. The owner of the bar, Leon, whom Nora had never met, had a reputation for sleeping with all the women he hired. Sleeping with Leon, at least once, was a condition of the job. He was in his late thirties, not particularly unattractive, and many of the women who applied for the job were desperate enough to go through the motions of making love to him on the floor of his office if it meant that he would hire them. It didn't take long, really, the sex part, five, ten minutes. And if it meant so much to him, as it seemed to, then there was nothing wrong with it. Their own reputations weren't going to suffer because they'd slept with him to get the job. There was even something exciting about making love on the carpeted rug in the office in the back of the bar. It didn't mean undressing, either. All you had to do was close your eyes and pretend it wasn't happening.

Kathy admitted that it was a form of prostitution to fuck someone in order to get something in return. It excited her while it was happening, but afterward she felt demeaned by it all. At least that's what she told her friend Nora who lived across the street from the bar. She told Nora that while it was happening she wanted to kill him, get a gun and point it to the side of his head and pull the trigger. Yet the odd thing, at least it seemed odd to Nora, was that a week or two after Kathy began working at the bar she began going out with Leon after the bar closed. They would go to restaurants or dancing or to hear music at an after-hours club near the Holland Tunnel that Leon knew about. There was a rumor among the other waitresses that Leon had fallen in love with Kathy, that he was planning to leave his family so he and Kathy could get a loft together, that he was paying her double what he was paying them, that he had offered to pay the entire rent of her apartment in exchange for sleeping with him. Sometimes Leon and Kathy would go to her apartment after the bar closed, sniff heroin, and fall asleep. They fell asleep on the couch, with their clothing on, listening to a tape of Billie Holiday singing "God Bless the Child" or Messiaen's "Quartet for the End of Time." Then he would wake up, suddenly, in a daze, usually the light at the window was what got him up, and he would rush off to his wife and children. He would take a cab to his apartment on the Upper East Side where he lived with his family.

Nora had the feeling that her friend Kathy was falling in love with the owner of the bar. She was tempted to apply for a job there herself just to have the experience of turning him down when he propositioned her. She wondered whether she would have the strength. Kathy had told her that the day she applied for the job he had walked around from behind his desk and had stood behind her chair. He had placed his hands on her shoulders, lightly, talking all the time. He never stopped talking, massaging her back, he had a beautiful voice. He could seduce anyone with that voice. She could feel the tension easing from her neck and shoulders. Nora wondered how Kathy felt whenever a new waitress was hired. Did it make her jealous? The longest anyone ever worked at Leon's was six months so he was always hiring new women, new girls. Nora couldn't understand why none of the women who applied for work at the bar ever complained about Leon's behavior. But who could they complain to? He never came out and said "If you want the job

18

you have to sleep with me — now," but the message was implied. He wasn't forcing you to do something you didn't want to do. It was common knowledge that you had to sleep with him to get the job. You were free to walk out of his office at any time.

Nora wondered how many job applicants had turned down his offer. "I wanted to spit in his face," Kathy told her. At this point she had been working in the bar for about a month. But if she feels this way, Nora thought, then why did she sleep with him again? "He's not really a bad guy," Kathy told her friend, unaware of the contradiction. "You should meet him." She sat alone at the end of the bar counting receipts, waiting for Leon to emerge from his office. They returned to her apartment almost every night. She would put on a record by Dinah Washington that he liked a lot. Sometimes he complained of a headache and she brought him an aspirin and a glass of water. "He's different from all the other men I've known," she said to Nora. "Every night we're together is different. Sometimes we just take off our clothes and sit on the couch without touching. Some nights we shoot up and fall asleep on the couch. Other times...." It was true, Nora thought, she's in love with him, but she isn't suffering.

Tom dialed her number, lying in bed in his brother's apartment with the phone against his ear, counting the rings. She had disconnected both the phone and the answering machine, as she sometimes did when they were making love. Her mother was sick, lived in another state, and she worried, when the phone rang late at night, that it was someone calling to tell her that her mother had died. A stranger's voice, a doctor or nurse she had never seen. Her mother was seventy-five years old and lived in a nursing home in a small town near the ocean where she had many friends. Whenever Nora spoke to her mother she felt guilty for not giving her more attention, for not visiting more frequently. Her mother was always careful never to say anything to make her daughter feel guilty. She assumed that Nora had better things to do than devote her life to nursing a sick old woman. There was no reason for her to do it.

Nora's mother had lived a full life and wasn't frightened of dying. She hated the pain that accompanied the disease, the loss of concentration and mobility, but she could still take pleasure in looking out the window at the ocean or listening to music, especially opera.

Nora visited her mother in North Carolina every three months and talked to her on the phone every week. It was a pleasure to visit her since it meant that Nora could spend a few days near the ocean as well. It was almost a vacation. One night, after a particularly grueling day with her mother in the nursing home, she went for a walk on the beach and met two men. She made love to both of them, willingly, desiring to give pleasure, the sound of the waves crashing against the shore in her ears. It was a way of wiping out all thoughts of illness and death, of transcending the inevitability of dying, at least for the moment. Anonymous sex is often more exciting than sex with someone you know. Nora knew that she wasn't the only person who felt this way. She wished that the scene on the beach with the two young men would go on forever. She hadn't gone to the beach with the thought of meeting someone. It had been her idea to make love, to fuck right there on the beach, not theirs. They would never have dared try anything if she hadn't reassured them that she wasn't planning to call the police afterwards and accuse them of raping her. That she wouldn't lose her nerve once it began.

The doctor in the nursing home had told her that her mother had an infection on the heel of her right foot that was possibly life-threatening. In order to prevent the poison from spreading they would have to amputate her mother's right leg. The doctor touched the place right below his own knee. "We'll have to cut it off here if we want to save her." Nora was an only child. Her father had died when she was fifteen (the day after she lost her virginity) and none of her mother's brothers and sisters were still alive. The decision whether the doctor should amputate her mother's leg was up to her. "If we don't amputate," the doctor said, looking out the window at the ocean, "she could die any time." Nora knew she would have to decide before she returned to the city. She called Tom, the man she'd been living with for the last ten years, but he wasn't home. Tom and her mother had never gotten along and he never accompanied her when she made her trips to North Carolina. She heard his voice on the answering machine and hung up without leaving a message.

Nora assumed that Tom slept with other women when she went to North Carolina. It was the only time that they were really separate from one another. She couldn't believe that he had remained faithful to her for the ten years they had been living together. Sometimes she asked him whether he ever felt like sleeping with someone else and he just shrugged. "Aren't you tired of me, yet?" she would say, turning it into a joke. She stood in the outdoor phonebooth facing the motel near the ocean listening to the waves of static inside the receiver. Then she heard Tom's voice on the machine and she said: "It's me, I'm still in North Carolina. I may have to stay longer than I planned." Maybe she would call him back later? She went down to the beach, it was after midnight, and met the two men. They were walking in her direction. There was no way they were going to pass one another on the beach without talking. She could see the outline of their bodies in the sand. She had to convince them that there was nothing to be nervous about. It wasn't the first time she had been with two men. One of the men seemed more willing to make love than the other. They were both still in college. One of them entered her while the other looked on. One of them was strong, a weight-lifter, maybe six and a half feet tall. Both of them had blonde, shoulder-length hair, just like her. It was a clear night, filled with constellations, and the moon was almost full.

She assumed that Tom had gone to the bar across the street for some company. She didn't blame him for feeling lonely when she was visiting her mother. Kathy, the waitress, had told her that the last time Nora had gone to visit her mother, Tom had come to the bar every night trying to convince her to go back with him to the apartment after work. It was on a night when the owner of the bar was sick, or so he said, home with his wife, and Kathy was angry at him. Obviously, no matter what he said, he had no intention of ever leaving his wife. Also, Leon had just hired a new waitress named Samantha and he was interested in her as well. For one thing, she was prettier and younger than Kathy, and seemed to be popular among the regular customers. So when Tom came into the bar that night when Nora was in North Carolina and Leon was at home with his wife she just shrugged her shoulders as if she were inwardly resigning herself to her own fate and leaned towards him so that her breasts were touching his arm and told him she would be happy to go with him to the apartment after she closed up. He waited on a stool at the end of the bar, nursing his drink. He helped her draw down the shutters over the windows of the bar. The apartment was a third floor walkup across the street. They sat on the futon in the living room, smoking, listening to music, nodding out a bit. Then Tom lifted her in his arms and carried her into the bedroom, to the bed which he and Nora had shared for ten years. They stayed in bed until three o'clock the next afternoon.

"Tom's a wonderful lover," Kathy told Nora when she returned from North Carolina. They were sitting together in a booth at the back of the bar. It was almost closing time and the owner, Leon, emerged from his office. "I want you to meet someone," Kathy said. She kicked Nora's leg under the table. Leon slid into the booth and kissed Kathy on the neck. "Stop it," she said playfully, but Leon didn't stop. He squeezed Kathy's breasts without looking at Nora. "Not here," Kathy said. "Later."

Nora walked across the street and climbed the steps to her apartment. She took off her clothes, slipped her nightgown over her head, drank a small tumbler of peach nectar and brushed the tartar from her gums. When she got into bed, Tom woke up briefly and she draped her arm around his waist, resting her chin against his naked shoulder. "I was dreaming about you," he said, without opening his eyes.

PICKUP ON TENTH STREET

It was after midnight, a Wednesday, the bar was almost empty. Three women in their early thirties came in laughing and sat down at a booth. One of the women, Teresa, stood up almost immediately and announced to her friends that she was going to the bathroom, which was located behind a glass door and down a flight of stairs. On her way, she smiled at a man sitting alone at a table.

"Don't I know you?" she asked.

He shrugged, "Maybe," looking straight at her without recognition, taking her words literally and thinking, "no, I don't *know* you," and said, finally, "Can I buy you a drink?"

The woman leaned over his table and said, "I'll be right back." She walked down the hallway, the steps, opened the bathroom door, and stared at herself in the mirror. Took the brush from her pocketbook and lifted her hair from one shoulder and held it up to the light inspecting for split ends. One of the other women, one of her friends, Alison, came into the bathroom and stood directly behind her in the mirror. She put her hands on Teresa's breasts and buried her face in her hair. She tried to sneak a hand under her skirt but Teresa pushed it away.

She had already told Alison that she wasn't going to go home with her that night but Alison didn't want to hear about it and Teresa was frightened of inciting her anger. That's why she was letting her touch her breasts, now, in the bathroom, the straps of her bra sliding down her arms. She actually didn't mind fooling around outside, it excited her more than if they were back in her apartment, but she didn't say this to Alison. She kind of let it all glide for a few minutes, reciprocating by slipping her hand down the front of Alison's blouse and squeezing her nipple. She promised Alison that they would spend a night together next week.

"I can't wait," Alison said.

She went into one of the stalls and pulled down her pants without closing the door and Teresa, resisting the temptation to watch, took advantage of the moment of freedom to leave the bathroom and go upstairs.

The man at the table — blonde, mustache, no tie — was waiting for her. He had already ordered her a drink.

"I took the liberty...." She waved her hand. It wasn't necessary for him to explain. She pulled the chair away from the table and crossed her legs, skirt pulled up, her knees touching his.

Christina and Alex came into the bar holding hands. Christina put a quarter into the jukebox and played "Tonight, Tonight" by the Mellowkings but it didn't come on immediately. They sat at a booth in the corner, ordered two beers, and Christina told him how bored she had been earlier in the summer before he arrived. It had not been a very productive year, to say the least.

"One night," she said, "about a month ago, I was so restless I came here at about midnight and picked up this guy, a total stranger. He lived right around the corner on Tenth Street. It wasn't a bad apartment, two bedrooms, a small living room, a kitchen and a full tile bath, and I could almost imagine living there with him, cooking his meals, but he said 'Do you want to watch a movie?' and I said 'That's not what I came here for,' and he said 'But I'm not interested in women, I don't fuck women.' He said that many of his best friends were women. He said that when he first met a woman she assumed that they would eventually become lovers, that that's what he wanted as well. They were shocked and disappointed when he told them that he'd never been with a woman before. I was on the verge of falling asleep from the effort of trying to deny what he was telling me — the last thing I wanted was to be anyone's friend — when his roommate walked in and I asked them if they were lovers and they stared at their feet and the guy I met in the bar said 'Sometimes.' And then I asked the roommate if he liked women and he said 'Yes' so I made it with him."

"What an asshole she is," Alison said. She emptied the last of her beer into a glass, swallowed it, made a face, and waved to the bartender to get his attention.

The bartender, who was watching television, saw the woman waving at him from the booth. He ignored her. There was no table service; even an idiot could see that. If she wanted a drink she'd have to get it herself.

Greta, who had met Alison and Teresa at a party the night before, hummed along to the song on the jukebox, "Devil or Angel" by the Clovers.

"You can have my beer," she said to Alison, tilting the bottle over the empty glass.

Greta's mother was German, but she had grown up in Fort Lauderdale, Florida. A year after her mother died, when she was twelve, she witnessed a murder from her bedroom window. She had identified the murderer to the police, a friend of her father's, but the lawyer for this man offered her father a large sum of money if he could convince her not to testify in court. A few months after her mother died her father introduced her to his new girlfriend. Apparently he'd been seeing this woman even when Greta's mother was alive. Her name was Molly Stone, and she had two sons, Harry and Darryl. Molly slept over at Greta's house almost every night. One evening her father called Greta into the living room — Molly Stone and her sons were there — and tried to persuade her to go to the police and tell them she had been mistaken about the murder. That the man she had seen kill the woman with the icepick in the driveway of their apartment building was not Amos Akindo, as she had previously thought. He told her that he himself would call the police and tell them his daughter had made a mistake. She didn't have to do anything. He tried to persuade her by saying that he had been playing pool with Amos the night of the murder. Greta knew in her heart he was lying to save his friend and that he depended on her to lie as well; she knew nothing, at the time, about the money which Amos's lawyer had offered. She felt no particular loyalty towards her father, only a kind of fear of what he might do if she didn't go along with his plan. She hated him mostly for being unfaithful to the memory of her mother. It was Darryl who eventually told Greta that her father and Molly had been going out together for over a year before Greta's mother had died.

"I wish I was a stronger person," she confessed to Alison. "I wish I hadn't listened to him."

Greta's father used the money which Amos Akindo's lawyer gave him to take his family north, put a down payment on a house in a suburb of Boston, and purchase a share of the Oldsmobile dealership where he now worked. By this time her father and Molly Stone were married. Greta told Alison that she occasionally dreamed about the man with the icepick (Amos Akindo) and the young woman whom he had picked up earlier that night in a bar, seventeen years old, her short white party dress covered with blood. Greta had many friends in Fort Lauderdale and one boy, especially, with whom she thought she was in love, as much as she knew anything about love, and the last thing she wanted to do was move to a strange city, the last thing she wanted was a life that involved Molly Stone and her two slovenly sons. She didn't like the way the two young men looked up from their magazines when she entered a room; she couldn't sit in the same room with them without feeling they were undressing her in their minds.

One night, a month after they moved to the house in Boston, a month after they began living under the same roof in the three bedroom house where Molly and her father shared one bedroom and the two brothers shared another and Greta was given the small-est room, a maid's room really, no bigger than a large closet, the older brother Harry returned home drunk late one night and tried to get into bed with her, lifting her nightgown under the blanket and then climbing on top of her. She managed to push him aside, clawing his cheek with her fingernails (drawing blood) and escape down a ladder that was leaning against the side of the house. She told Alison how the next day, when she complained to her father about what Harry Stone had done, he laughed in her face.

Teresa said, "I told you I knew you," and Victor said, "It's pos-sible. I didn't believe you at first."

She said: "You thought it was a line."

"I've used it myself," Victor said, "but not recently."

After five minutes of talk, they discovered that they were the same age, born only five days apart, and that they had attended the same college in upstate New York. Neither had graduated, though Teresa had lasted a year longer. She told him that she had lived for five years, the length of her marriage, in Santa Fe, New Mexico. He knew the street that she lived on and the bar named Claude's where she worked as a waitress. After her marriage ended, she said, she moved back east. Victor asked her about the courses she had taken in college: possibly they had been in the same class? He mentioned the name of a professor in the psychology department but she shook her head.

He told her that he lived a few blocks away, just below Houston, but that he didn't like his apartment, he was thinking of moving to Brooklyn to a bigger place, that he had two cats, that he'd been married, once, as well, and though it had ended five years ago he was still getting over it in the sense that he assumed now that all relationships were doomed, that nothing ever lasts, and that it was pointless to get overly involved with anyone with the hope that it might go on forever. It was the "forever" part that created the pres-sure on most people who lived together. He knew he was dominating the conversation but he had the sense that she was interested, that she was relating to what he was saying. As he talked, he was aware of her knee pressing against his thigh.

Teresa knew that Alison was probably angry with her for leaving her alone with Greta. As a way of retaliating, they — Alison and Greta — would probably go home together. In Teresa's mind this turn of events wasn't the worst thing that could happen. Alison had assured her over the phone that Greta didn't even like women, that she was lonely and wanted friends. Alison had stopped sleeping with men and couldn't understand why Teresa still bothered. She had been contemplating asking Teresa whether she wanted to move in with her. It was stupid for each of them to pay $800 a month for their tiny apartments. The only reason to sleep with a man, as far as Alison was concerned, was to make babies. If that was the reason, she wouldn't mind if Teresa slept with someone (a man), but that was the only reason. She had a fantasy of being in the delivery room while Teresa was giving birth, of holding her hand, of breathing with her while she was in labor. The fact that men were even necessary to conceive a child was, from Alison's point of view, a crime against nature.

"Did you know Renee Jacobson?" Teresa asked.

"Of course," Victor said. "She was Tom Pool's girlfriend."

She would mention a name and he would nod his head as a sign of recognition. She had had a hard time adjusting to life in college, to being away from her parents. Among her friends, she was the only one who was still a virgin. She didn't know how to drive a car or cook and she had never laundered her own clothing. She remembered spending her Saturday nights lying in her bed in her dormitory room composing letters to her parents and to her sister Marie. People were laughing in the hallways and outside in the quadrangle she could hear firecrackers and the sound of a radio playing "You Send Me" by Sam Cooke. In subsequent years, whenever she heard the song "You Send Me" she remembered that moment, how lonely she felt, how separate from everyone else.

Renee would come in at two in the morning after a date with Tom Pool. Sometimes Renee would ask Teresa whether she could spend the night elsewhere so that she and Tom could sleep together in the room. They had nowhere else to go. Renee arranged for her to sleep in a room down the hall; the girls who lived there were going away for the weekend. Once, during the week, Teresa woke up in the middle of the night to the sound of Renee and Tom fucking in the bed across the room. "They think I'm asleep," she said to herself, "or maybe they just don't care."

Edgar always came to the bar after fighting with his wife. He sat on a stool, in the corner near the door, ordered a beer, drank it straight from the bottle, and then another, all the time replaying the argument, everything he might have said if he hadn't walked out. If I don't care about what she does when she's not with me, he said to himself, then I won't feel this way, right? It wasn't simply a rationalization but a plan, a way of being, that actually made some sense. If I only think about what I do, at all times, and not concern myself with what she's thinking or doing, or who she might be with — something I'll never know anyway — then I'll never have to feel this way again. He felt like he needed a tourniquet or a giant band-aid to stop the pain.

He recognized that in his previous marriage the same thing had happened: he had driven his first wife away with his insecurity, his jealousy, his suspicion. But when his second wife accused him of being "crazy" (her word) for questioning what she did, he assumed (in the depth of his distrust for her) that saying this was the ultimate lie. I'm lying to you and if you don't believe me, you're the one who's crazy. He tried to deny that she was the type of person who would purposely try to hurt him. If she's lying and I know she's lying then it's my fault as well. He would accuse her of lying and she would accuse him of being crazy. She acted angry and resentful whenever he accused her of lying. Worst of all, Edgar knew that if he were ever unfaithful to her, he would say the same things.

When they first met, she already had a boyfriend, and he had waited, patiently, until she made her choice: him or me. He knew that she was sleeping with both of them, that she was capable of such a thing, but he managed — since they weren't living together yet — to hold that thought in abeyance, to keep his jealousy under control, to assume that what was happening was a prelude to the rest of their life together. (He refused to believe that she would some day repeat the same scenario with someone else.) He never once gave her an ultimatum — him or me, *now* — but let her play it through, the drama she loved so much, until finally she let her first boyfriend off the hook, told him the news, and showed up at Edgar's apartment one night, teary-eyed, suitcase in hand. They had been together for four years.

All his thoughts about their life together had nothing and everything to do with the pain in his heart. There was no way of thinking through a feeling so that it would eventually go away. Thinking never solved anything, yet it was all he had.

She had arrived home late, as she did every Wednesday night after class (the class ended at eight, she had returned at eleven-thirty), and he had asked her what she had done and she told him, as usual, that the teacher had kept them past the time the class normally ended, that she had to talk to the teacher after class about a paper she was writing, that she had gone out with a friend — a woman friend, she even mentioned a name — for something to eat, that the train was delayed and she had to wait for forty minutes at the 68th Street station, that she fell asleep on the train and missed her stop. All these excuses added up to how many hours? In her school notebook she had written a phone number and he had called it up one night and a man's voice on the answering machine said, "This is George, I'm not at home now, please leave a message." So there was the issue of this person George and who he might be. And then sometimes the phone rang when he was home and the person at the other end hung up. Once, a man asked to speak to his wife, who wasn't home, and when Edgar asked if he could take a message, the man said, "No, not necessary," and hung up. The asshole refused to even give his name, Edgar thought. So there was the lateness after class and the feeling that every time he left the house she left too, after him, that she was waiting for him to leave so she could go out to see — whoever!

Once, with his first wife, Yvonne, in an attempt to either appease or confirm his suspiciousness, he had decided to spy on her. He stood across the street from the office building where she worked. He watched her leave, holding the arm of a man he'd never seen before. He followed them for a few blocks until they reached the building where he lived (or so Edgar assumed), a high-rise with a doorman. She was with him for an hour. He watched her walk across the lobby, carrying her coat. "Enough time for a quick fuck," he muttered bitterly to himself, wanting to kill someone. As soon as the doorman saw her coming, he rushed out into the street, blew his whistle and flagged down a taxi. She was already home when he returned (Edgar had taken the subway) and when he asked her what she had done after work she said that she went to visit her mother. "Where were *you*?" she asked, diverting the suspicion. A typical ploy. He lit a cigarette, opened a beer and told her everything he had seen. She hung her head momentarily, anticipating punishment, a slap, the rush of footsteps which meant he was leaving. But he didn't say anything which was the worst punishment of all since she knew he was waiting for her to confess; she was cornered, she had no choice. After an endless unendurable silence, during which he finished his beer and lit another cigarette, she told him that she had been sleeping with her co-worker for the last six months, but that she wasn't in love with him. "What's his name?" Edgar was tempted to ask, but what difference did it make? In a flash, he remembered all the nights when she returned home late and presented him with her repertoire of excuses. He had believed her, he had wanted to believe her, he had denied that she was lying to preserve their life together. If nothing else, now that everything was out in the open, he had the vague satisfaction of knowing his instincts had been correct.

Of course his new wife Lydia knew what had happened with Yvonne, knew that she had been unfaithful to him, Edgar had told her everything. And now, when he expressed his jealousy, which took the form of anger, saying the worst things that came into his head, she would turn to him and say:"I'm not Yvonne, don't confuse us. When you shout at me you're really shouting at her." Edgar knew that this was at least partially accurate but he also sensed that to say this was part of a complicated subterfuge that involved transferring the burden of guilt from her to him. What it always came down to was that he was the crazy one. "Why don't you follow me like you did with her?" Lydia would say. He knew that he would feel the same way about any woman, that he was attracted to women who had the potential to deceive him, but that it was also possible for Lydia — or whoever — to give him a sense of reassurance so that he didn't have to experience the torments of jealousy, especially if there was no reason. He wasn't sure, exactly, what she could do to make it clear to him that she wasn't lying, but he wanted her to do something.

And meanwhile, there was always this bar, where he could slow down, take a break, watch his thoughts come and go, one thought bleeding into another, as if he were observing himself from a distance, this is me feeling these things. The last thing he wanted was to go through life repeating what he had done before. The last thing he wanted was to feel like a victim, a person whose nervous system was dependent on what someone else did.

And the only way out, it always came down to the same thing, was to live his own life irrespective of anyone else. Even the person you married, this person you called your wife or husband, was a separate being. It was a dumb illusion on his part to think you could be connected so intensely to anyone else, yet it was what he wanted, not the illusion but the luminous thread of longing that extended to infinity. The impossibility of it all, with anyone, ever, was the source of his strange sadness.

"I want another beer," Christina said.

Alex was due at the airport at seven the next morning. That's when his plane back to California was scheduled to leave. He assumed, since it was already almost one, that he would stay awake all night. It was pointless to insist on going to sleep and then wake up exhausted, as exhausted as he might be if he never slept at all. His plan was to take a seconal and sleep on the plane, close his eyes in New York (while the plane was still on the ground) and wake up five hours later as it was circling above San Francisco Bay.

He had come to New York three weeks before to see a publisher who was interested in a book of his stories and to visit with his father who was recovering from open heart surgery. Before leaving California, his wife Arlette had called her friend Christina to ask whether she had room in her apartment for Alex to stay. Christina and Arlette had known each other since high school. During this long distance phone conversation between Arlette and Christina, Alex hovered in the background, not certain whether he was really happy with the arrangement. In his imagination, he had seen himself in a hotel room on the Upper East Side, looking out over the city, drink in hand. It would be his reward for selling the book, but Arlette thought differently. Look at all the money he'd save if he stayed with Christina. Be practical for once in your life.

The last thing Alex imagined was that he and Christina would become lovers. For the first week, he slept on an air mattress on her living room floor. There was only one bedroom in the apartment, only one proper bed. Every afternoon Alex went uptown by subway to the hospital where his father was recovering from his operation. Alex's stepmother usually visited in the evening, after work, and Alex wanted to avoid seeing her. As soon as he arrived in New York, he called up all his old friends. He had dinner at their homes or met them in restaurants or bars for drinks, but after five years there was no way he could re-enter their lives in any real way.

Most nights he spent alone in Christina's apartment, watching the news on TV or one of her many tapes, until she returned home from her film classes at New York University. One night a week she worked for an escort service; she accompanied men, mostly elderly or middle-aged, to cocktail parties, or to the opera. She was writing a screenplay about a young woman, much like herself, who worked for an escort service, and what happened when one of the men fell in love with her. Christina told Alex that after an hour or two the man she was with tended to forget that she had been hired to go out with him and began to think she was willingly providing her services because she enjoyed his company. Sometimes, if she liked the guy, she would give him a blowjob in the back of the cab on the way to his hotel. It was rare for one of these men not to assume that she would eventually go to bed with him.

Often, before falling asleep, Alex and Christina watched a movie together on Christina's bed. They saw *The Manchurian Candidate*, *400 Blows*, *Suddenly Last Summer*. One night they both fell asleep in front of the VCR fully dressed and woke up in each other's arms. They removed their clothing in slow motion and made love like zombies in the dawn light, with Christina on top. Since then they slept together every night, easing into one another's arms as the characters in the movie they were watching faded into oblivion. Christina had never lived with anyone who was always there when she came home. There was no need to tell one another how they spent their respective days, no need to talk. She undressed in front of the full-length mirror on the door of her closet while Alex watched her from the bed. She knelt alongside him, taking his cock in her mouth. She buried her face in the pillow and spread her legs. "Slap my ass," she ordered, as Alex hovered over her. It was something that Arlette had never permitted him to do.

"If you want," Christina said, as they were sitting in the bar, "I'll call up Arlette and tell her what happened. I'll tell her we fell in love and want to live together forever."

"In My Diary" by the Moonglows was playing on the jukebox.

As Alex approached the bar to get more beer he noticed a couple in the back, in the space between tables, dancing to the music. He saw the woman's golden hair as she tilted her head to be kissed. He noticed the two women, surrounded by empty beer bottles and ashtrays, sitting at a booth holding hands. One of the women was crying while the other was attempting to comfort her. He noticed a man with a beard, perched on a stool near the door, drinking beer from a thin-necked bottle that seemed as long as the arm that was holding it. When the bartender came by to take his order, Alex pointed to the bottle which the man was caressing and said: "I'll take one of those."

SWEET SIXTEEN

They were driving south on Route 13 through Maryland and Virginia when a blonde shirtless young man appeared with his thumb in the air on the side of the road. Elizabeth guided the car onto a strip of gravel fifty yards ahead of where he was standing, rested her arms on the steering wheel, and stared at his figure in the rearview mirror. As the man ran towards the car, dragging his duffel bag on the ground behind him, Maureen turned to her friend, adjusted her skirt over her knees, and said: "I trust your instincts, but he looks like a killer." The hitch-hiker opened the back door, threw his duffel bag onto the seat, and climbed in.

"Thanks for stopping," he said, in a way that made it sound like he was doing them a favor by accepting the ride. "How far you going?"

As Elizabeth eased the car into the flow of traffic, the hitch-hiker leaned forward, looking over the front seat at the bodies of the two women, trying not to be obvious but wanting them to know what he was doing. He carried with him the smell of pine cones or maple syrup, something musky, like he'd been rolling around naked on the ground.

Elizabeth told him that they were heading for the North Carolina coast, the area known as The Outer Banks, a town called Nag's Head where her parents owned a house. They were going to spend a week in a house near the ocean.

For a few minutes they drove in silence, like characters in a pornographic movie, the two young women in short dresses up front, the bare-chested young man in the back looking out the window. What he saw when he looked were farms, some of them deserted, cornfields and vegetable stands, an occasional billboard warning of the evils of television — how it corrupted the morals of young people and would eventually lead to the end of the world. Then Maureen turned around and asked him where he was from. It was the usual question that a driver or passenger asks a hitch-hiker but she couldn't think of what else to say.

"Canada," he said, mentioning the name of a city or province where neither Elizabeth nor Maureen had ever been.

Elizabeth, who had driven this route before, told them about a 25-mile long bridge spanning Chesapeake Bay and Maureen took out her Minolta and said she wanted to take some photographs when they crossed. Elizabeth didn't know how long it would be before they reached the bridge but she hoped it would still be light out. The hitch-hiker, who hadn't told them his name or how far he was traveling, asked to see the camera and Maureen handed it back to him.

"I used to have one of these," he said.

He focused on the back of Maureen's head and when she turned in his direction he snapped her picture.

"Hey," she said, "don't do that." She tried to sound annoyed, but she was smiling. "I look horrible."

From time to time, during the drive, Elizabeth and Maureen stared at one another covertly, or so they thought, trying to communicate their feelings and impressions about the hitch-hiker without using words. Already they could imagine the dingy motel room where the three of them would spend the night: the glow of the TV, the spray of the shower on their backs, the smell of the sheets as they spread their legs.

They stopped for late lunch at a roadside diner called The Paradise Grill and Elizabeth and Maureen were surprised that the hitch-hiker, whose name was Eddie (at least that's what he told them) had enough money to pay for himself. Before entering the restaurant, he fished in his bag for a clean workshirt which he buttoned up in the restaurant parking lot and tucked into his pants. They sat in a booth covered with blotchy chartreuse upholstery which stuck to their thighs, the two women facing him, and during the meal (omelets, cheeseburgers, French fries, milkshakes) Elizabeth felt the pressure of his foot against her ankle. Then his knee touched her knee, pressing against it firmly, and she didn't move away, but parted her legs slightly and pressed back, smiling at him. Over cigarettes and coffee he began to open up, telling them about the one time in his life he'd been in New York and how he got lost on the subway and ended up in Brooklyn. "So you're from Brooklyn?" he said, shaking his head, as if he couldn't believe people actually lived in such a place. "To me," he said, "it's just a place to get lost in, not to see." Elizabeth said that the next time he came to New York she'd give him a tour of the city. He slouched in his seat, the leg of his jeans scratching the inside of her thigh, and told them that his parents had died in an auto accident when he was ten, and that's when he moved from Florida (where he was born, where he was heading) to Canada (where he was coming from) to live with relatives. As he talked, bumming one cigarette after another from Elizabeth's pack of Kool Lights, Maureen thought: I don't believe a word, it's all a big mistake. She could sense something was going on between the hitch-hiker and her friend (the way he lit her cigarette, the way he addressed his words mainly to her), and she was jealous.

It was raining when they left the restaurant and Eddie offered to drive. They had stayed in the restaurant longer than they had planned and would never reach the bridge before dark. The car was a brand new Chrysler Le Baron which Elizabeth had rented in New York with her American Express card. It was silver, with gray trim, her favorite colors. Elizabeth sat up front and Maureen moved to the backseat. She fell asleep and Eddie took Elizabeth's hand and held it between them on the front seat as he steered with the other. Every few minutes she lit a cigarette with the dashboard lighter, one for herself, one for him. Maureen was still asleep, her head resting against Eddie's duffel bag. The rain had stopped, but the sky was one immense cloud, and some of the drivers passing in the opposite direction had already turned on their brights. There was a station on the radio playing songs from the fifties and sixties, music by groups of black women with names like the Shirelles and the Chiffons and the Ronettes, music that had been popular before Elizabeth, Maureen and Eddie were born.

Elizabeth asked him what movies he liked and he said he didn't like movies much he liked sports if he liked anything and so she said "What sports?" and he said "Volleyball" though he'd never played it and Elizabeth said that she'd been the captain of the volleyball team when she was in high school and he said "You don't seem tall enough" and she said "I was the tallest person on my team." As if to prove a point, she pulled the hem of her short print dress above her thighs and shifted her legs in his direction. He reached out and put his hand on her knee and looked at her for a moment, taking his eyes off the road just as a truck passed in the opposite direction with its brights shining in Eddie's face, blinding him slightly and forcing him to grab the steering wheel with both hands and turn it to the right to prevent a head-on collision. Elizabeth laughed, pulled her dress down, and straightened her legs so that her knees hit against the dashboard. When he offered his hand again she made a circle in his palm with her finger.

Elizabeth and Maureen had met when they were sophmores in high school and now they were going to be seniors in college and they were still friends. They had gone to different colleges but had stayed in touch. Elizabeth remembered at the end of their junior year in high school when Maureen called her up late one night to tell her she was no longer a virgin. She remembered enduring a lengthy description of what it had been like to make love to her boyfriend Alex, how she had been drunk but not drunk enough to know what they were doing. Maureen insisted that she had enjoyed it, that she was in love with Alex, that they were going to apply to the same college and live together in an apartment off-campus, none of which ever happened. Elizabeth remembered the night Maureen called her up from college to tell her she was pregnant, that she was going to have the baby, and then calling her back the next night to say she was going to get an abortion. The towns where they were going to college, in upstate New York, were only fifty miles apart. Elizabeth picked up Maureen on the steps of her dormitory and drove her to the abortion clinic and waited in a lounge filled with comfortable threadbare sofas and armchairs and a brown majogany coffeetable with piles of magazines: *Vogue, The New Yorker*. There was only one other person in the lounge, a woman in her mid-thirties with prematurely white hair who was wearing a ring in the shape of a snake that curled the length of her middle finger. Elizabeth, unable to concentrate on her German lesson (she had an exam the next day) asked if she could see it. The woman, who was wearing sunglasses and turning the pages of a magazine with glossy reproductions of Renaissance paintings, looked up and smiled. "It's just some cheap ring I bought on the street," she said, crossing her legs. "You can have it if you like."

Eddie told her that his father had been in the army and that they had lived (he, his parents, and two sisters) in various army bases in the southwestern part of the United States until he was ten and the accident happened. He said the word "accident" and swallowed and then didn't say anything, forcing Elizabeth to ask: "What accident?" which is what he had intended her to do, giving him time to make up the story as he went along. Apparently his parents were driving home from a party with another couple and they were hit by a truck. Everyone died, including the truck driver. After that he was sent to live with his mother's brother in the city he had mentioned earlier, Port Elgin, on the coast of Lake Huron. Elizabeth moved closer to him, not knowing how much she believed of his story, not caring.

They were still a hundred miles from the house in Nag's Head when the cat leapt in front of the car. Eddie pressed down hard on the brakes and Maureen fell forward out of sleep and hit her forehead on the back of the seat. Each of them had heard a thud, the contact of the fender or tire with the body of an animal, but neither of them suggested they stop to see if the animal was alive. It could have been a raccoon or a skunk, but it had looked to both Eddie and Elizabeth like a big cat with bright eyes, more like a leopard or a cougar. Elizabeth wished she could be alone with Maureen, if only for a moment, so she could tell her everything she was feeling.

"I'm sorry I stopped so suddenly," Eddie apologized. "Are you O.K.?"

The motel was called Whispering Pines. It consisted of a dozen connected units, one story high, with a slanted tile roof, modest red brick in an L-shape around a tiny swimming pool. There was a grove of exhausted weather-beaten pinetrees behind the motel. A beachchair had fallen over onto the grass alongside the pool and some purple and yellow leaves floated on the water's surface. Maureen went into the office and paid for a room with her Visa card. As soon as they were alone in the car (it was the first time they had ever been alone), Eddie put his hand between Elizabeth's legs, biting down gently on her lower lip as his finger moved inside her. In the office of the motel a woman in pin curlers ("dead batteries" as they were called when Maureen and Elizabeth were in high school) asked how many people were going to sleep in the room and without hesitating Maureen said: "Two, me and my friend." Maureen asked the manager of the motel if there was any place nearby where she could buy some food. It was almost nine o'clock and everyone was hungry again. The manager told her that there was a strip of restaurants about a mile down the road: Bob's Big Boy, Hardees, KFC, Burger King, MacDonalds, Pizza Hut, Taco Bell. One after the other, maybe a drive-in bank or an auto supply store in between. Maureen didn't bother getting back into the car but pointed to Eddie to follow her to their room. He stopped the car outside the door which Maureen had opened and helped Elizabeth unpack the trunk, what they'd need for the night. Maureen offered to drive down the road to buy some food and bring it back to the room.

"You don't mind?" Elizabeth asked. "Shouldn't we all go?"

Maureen winked at her.

"Don't worry about me," she said. "Think about yourself for a change."

She went into the bathroom and locked the door behind her. She peeled the wrapper off a miniature bar of Ivory soap and washed her hands. Rubbed skin moisturizer over her face, put on lipstick, blush and mascara, changed from her white dress into jeans and a tank top. When she emerged from the bathroom fifteen minutes later, Eddie was sitting on the floor in front of the TV watching the Olympic Games, looking bored. Elizabeth was lying on the bed behind him. She was leaning back against the wall, skirt tucked between knees, brushing her hair.

Maureen drove past the strip of fast food restaurants. About a mile further down the road she saw a sign, Little Anthony's, and turned into the parking lot. She could hear a woman laughing out of control from a car parked nearby and music from the door of the bar, not live music, but a jukebox turned on full blast. The people in the bar were laughing and dancing. It was Saturday night. Most of the women in the bar were in their late twenties and wore long frilly cowgirl dresses or tight jeans with crocheted blouses. Many of them were divorced from their husbands and lived alone with their children and worked during the week while their children were in school. Some of them had dyed their hair to make them look younger. The men wore cowboy hats or baseball caps and didn't seem to pay much attention to the way they looked. Some of them had beards, some of them needed shaves, others were obviously more interested in drinking than dancing or picking up women. There was a group of men sitting at a table at the far end of the bar playing cards. There were women of all ages, though none as young as Maureen, carrying pitchers of beer and bowls of chips on trays and laughing with the customers who stood at the dance floor when the music came on.

Maureen found a place at the bar and ordered a Jack Daniels with ice. At the sound of her voice, obviously she wasn't from around here, the man to her right turned a full circle and tipped his hat. He asked her where she was from and she said New York City and he told her that he had been in New York a year ago to visit his sister who lived in Brooklyn. Saying you were from New York always inspired some kind of response. The top three buttons of his denim shirt were open. He was wearing a wide leather belt with a gold buckle and his face twitched slightly. When he caught her noticing his tic he said: "I do that when I'm nervous." He had a tattoo of a rose on his left wrist. His hair was thinning. He wore a ring that looked like a wedding band and when Maureen asked him if he was married he said his wife was dead. He smiled when he said it and Maureen felt like laughing in his face. She sipped her drink and he ordered another beer, calling the bartender by his first name. As she stared into her drink Maureen saw the faces of her friend Elizabeth and the young man named Eddie whom they had picked up hitch-hiking. She saw Elizabeth's black hair spread out on the pillow. She saw their bodies, surrounded by a silver glow, moving rhythmically on the unmade bed. Then a person who was a friend or acquaintance of the man at the bar came up from behind him and slapped him on the shoulder and said, "Why don't you introduce me to your friend," motioning to Maureen, but the first man, whose name was Rex, said: "I would, but I don't know her name," and Maureen smiled as his face jumped again and said "I'm Maureen," and the second man offered his hand and said, "I'm Davis, nice to meet you." Maureen guessed that both these men were twice her age, forty or more, though she also knew that people who drank a lot usually looked older than they were. A Randy Travis song was playing on the jukebox and the man named Davis asked Maureen if she wanted to dance. She put down her glass on the bar, it was almost empty, anyway, and glanced back at Rex, whose face was going crazy. She rested her head on Davis's shoulder and could feel his breath against her cheek. It was a familiar smell, beer and smoke, but she didn't want to kiss him, not yet. He placed his hand on the small of her back and guided her in a slow circle around the dancefloor, gyrating slowly with his hips to see if she would respond. Maureen pressed him closer, her hands on his ass. Then the first man, Rex, came up to them, pushing his way through the crowd of dancers, holding a beer bottle by the neck, and tapped Davis on the shoulder. "My turn, friend," he said, though it was obvious he wasn't feeling very friendly. Davis looked at Rex with disgust and then at Maureen and said, "I'll be back, sweetheart, that's a promise," as if she cared one way or the other about either of them. A minute later the dance ended and a fast song came on and Rex, who had stepped on her toes twice, said: "I don't dance fast." He took her arm and tried to steer her back to the bar, but she slipped free and stood on the edge of the dancefloor watching a black man and a younger white girl with blonde hair down to her waist. The black man was the only non-white person in the bar as far as Maureen could tell. He lifted the young girl in his arms and swung her around while the people on the sidelines stomped their feet and applauded. Then the man named Davis came up behind her and circled her waist with his arm. "It's my turn," he said to Maureen, kissing her on the side of the neck. "I'll show that nervous fucker how to dance."

APRÈS LE BAIN

"I wish I was marrying you instead of her," Richard said. He was sitting at the kitchen table in Deva's apartment drinking coffee from a porcelain cup she had brought back from Cancun. There was an empty vase, a glass ashtray, a container of skin milk, a box of Strike Anywheres, and a bowl of sugar on the wooden table.

Deva leaned back against the stove smoking a cigarette. She crossed her arms over her breasts and studied the back of Richard's head as he sipped his coffee. "You can still come over for lunch," she said in response to his remark about getting married. Richard worked as a clerk in a hardware store down the street from Deva's apartment and had been visiting her during his lunch hour, twice a week, for the last year and a half. He'd call at about ten, while she was still half-asleep, and ask if it was a good day for him to come over for lunch. "Lunch" meant going to bed together, it was the word they used to equate desire with hunger, and Deva couldn't remember ever saying no. It was a perfect arrangement, except that she had fallen in love with him, something she had promised herself she wouldn't do, and Richard had met someone else, a Swedish woman named Britta who worked as an assistant producer for *Good Morning America*, an early morning television program which Deva had never seen. One of the reasons he was marrying Britta was because she promised to support him so he could quit his hated job at the hardware store where he'd been working for three years. The convenience of the arrangement between Richard and Deva had something to do with the proximity of Richard's job to her apartment, but neither of them knew how much. When he told her that he was quitting his job on Friday and getting married on Saturday she was tempted to ask — *When will we see each other?* — but didn't. She could hear the desperation in her voice even before she opened her mouth.

Richard squinted morosely into the depths of the coffee cup. There was no handle on the cup and the heat of the coffee was burning his fingers. He remembered the day Deva told him about her trip to Cancun, how envious he had felt. "I've never been anywhere," he said, though this was only partially true. He'd spent a month in Alaska when his father was in the hospital, an afternoon in Tijuana, a weekend with a girlfriend whose parents owned a house in Key West. He was born in a suburb of Boston and had lived there with his mother and step-father until he was seventeen. Then he went to college in upstate New York but it was too cold so he transferred to a college in Jacksonville, Florida but never graduated (his stepfather once called him a "faggot" because he liked to read poetry). He and Britta were flying to Los Angeles after the wedding (she had to interview the wife of a soap opera star who had died in a boating accident) and then to Hawaii for a week. Richard wanted to stay longer, especially since her parents were paying for it all, but Britta was worried about losing her job.

He had assumed that this would be their last lunch hour together, that when he told Deva he was planning to get married she would end their relationship. Certainly, no one could blame her for not wanting to share him with someone else. Not only was he quitting his job but he was moving out of his studio apartment on Ludlow Street into Britta's co-op in the West 90s. It was a much larger apartment, with a terrace and a team of doormen patrolling the lobby, and he could have his own room, with a view of Central Park. If he and Deva wanted to see one another again it meant he would have to make a special trip downtown. It also meant that they were free of the parameters of the lunch hour ("Is it a good time?") which had previously defined their relationship. When she said that he could still come over whenever he liked, even though he was getting married, he turned in his chair and spilled the coffee down the front of his shirt. "Are you kidding?" he asked. Incredulous, child-like. Deva crossed the room with a paper towel and wiped the front of his shirt so it wouldn't stain. As she bent over him, Richard untied the belt of her robe and pressed the side of his face against her stomach. "I don't joke about things like this," Deva said. Britta, Richard was thinking, often left for work at six in the morning and didn't return home until seven or eight o'clock at night. Enough time to take the subway downtown to visit Deva whenever he wanted. If Britta called him at home he could always say he had gone for a walk in the park.

They were getting married on Saturday, in a town north of the city where Britta's parents owned a restaurant on a hill overlooking the Hudson. Both Britta and Deva were thirty years old. Richard was a year younger, but looked older than both of them. His hair was prematurely gray and he was beginning to put on weight. Since he met Britta, who didn't like to cook after working all day, who had grown up in a household where food and restaurant business was all anyone talked about, he had been eating out almost every night. "Too much restaurant food," he said, as he sucked in his stomach in front of Deva's mirror. The first time he visited Deva she had even prepared a real lunch for him, thinking that lunch meant eating food, and that he would be hungry after working all morning. But five minutes after he arrived they were rolling around on the kitchen floor. "Let's go into the bedroom," she had said, her willingness to comply registering as an aftershock to her own needs, "it'll be more comfortable." (After he left, and without realizing what she was doing, she sat at the kitchen table and devoured a bowl of avocado salad and a plate of prosciutto and melon, the food she had prepared for both of them and which neither had touched.) Sometimes they made love leaning against the kitchen table or sitting half-dressed in one of the kitchen chairs. He arrived at five minutes after twelve, out of breath from running up the three flights of stairs (anticipating the pleasure was part of the excitement), and she greeted him at the door in a nightgown or a robe or a slip. It was only the first half-hour that they could concentrate on making love; after that, she could tell he was thinking about having to leave. Sometimes they made love twice, quickly up against the stove or table, and then, a bit more leisurely, in her bed, ending with just enough time for him to pull up his pants, run down the stairs, and get back to his job.

In the days before he met Britta he had been concerned about alienating his boss at the hardware store. He hated the job, hated the wisecracks of his boss and his co-workers ("There must have been a special on pussy today") when he came in late, as if they could smell it on him or see Deva's reflection in his eyes, or read his mind. When Britta offered to support him, at least for a year while he worked on his stories, he realized that practical considerations, when it came to marriage, was as good a reason as being in love. In his past relationships, he had been the person who had fallen in love first, who had opened himself to the possibility of being hurt. And he had been hurt. Most of his previous girlfriends had deserted him for other lovers. He had the bad habit of falling in love with everyone he slept with. He couldn't imagine sleeping with someone and never seeing the person again. His girlfriends were often shocked at his willingness to commit himself to a relationship where the only thing in common was an interest in sex. All they had wanted was someone to sleep with for a single night — and here he was practically suggesting that they live together. His willingness to express his feelings, whether they were genuine or not, scared them away.

Britta didn't know how Richard spent his lunch hours. She had to wake at five to be in the TV studio before the show began. Her job, interviewing and researching pseudo-celebrities to determine whether they were suitable to appear on the show, was "all consuming," as Richard sometimes described it to Deva, and she was too distracted to keep track of how her future husband spent his days. Sometimes she didn't return home until eight at night. Working in television involved endless meetings, lunches, dinners. She had been attracted to Richard because he didn't seem like the type who would pressure her to choose between their life together and her job. He didn't need her attention, non-stop, the way other men did. Most of her previous boyfriends expected her to act like their mothers. Richard made it clear that he had no interest in sabotaging her career. Neither of them wanted children, not yet, anyway, if ever. She was anxious for him to quit his job at the hardware store. She offered to support him while he worked on his novel. She had read copies of the stories and poems he had written before they met and had decided, though she hardly qualified as a judge, that he had some talent. More than that, maybe. Her plan was to encourage him to write stories that were accessible to a lot of people. She fantasized about being married to the author of a best-selling novel. She wanted her husband to be someone who she could introduce to her friends at the TV station. Someone with stature. Maybe she could even help him get a job writing for a soap opera? She imagined herself as Richard's muse, the person to whom he would dedicate all his books. "For Britta, without whom nothing is possible," was her favorite imaginary dedication. Many of her friends from ABC were coming to the wedding and if any of them asked Richard what he did she prayed he would tell them he was a writer.

Britta had given him a set of keys to her apartment so he could go there after work. Either they'd meet back in her apartment or she'd call him at the store during the day. She always tried to call him at least once a day under the pretense of asking where he wanted to meet her for dinner. Richard preferred Indian food but Britta didn't like to travel downtown after work. She didn't want to go to Chinatown either. She insisted there were Chinese restaurants on the Upper West Side that were as good as the restaurants in Chinatown, but Richard knew this wasn't true. All the best Japanese restaurants were downtown as well. He eventually acquiesced: wherever you want to eat is fine with me. He felt like they had already been married twenty years and had exhausted every possible topic of conversation except what to eat for dinner and where to go. Some nights when they met at the restaurant of choice she would surprise him by ordering only an appetizer or a small salad. Apparently she'd already eaten something at the station — "I was starving, I couldn't wait" — and wasn't hungry. Richard preferred eating alone to eating with someone who was just drinking but he swallowed his food with alacrity and told her how good it was and brushed the crumbs from the corner of his mouth and offered her a taste and refilled her wineglass from the carafe he had ordered and poured a bit more for himself. He ate and drank continuously to avoid going crazy.

The apartment on Ludlow Street was one medium-sized room with a loftbed. There was a separate bathroom with a shower, a small kitchen alcove, high ceilings. The desk where he worked was an old door propped on gray filing cabinets. What he longed for most in life was a desk with drawers, maybe an old secretariat with numerous tiny compartments where he could file all his papers. He and Britta would walk passed an antique furniture store and Richard would point out a desk he liked and she would say, "Let me buy it for you." Britta couldn't believe that he still wrote his stories on a manual typewriter. She promised to buy him a word processor and teach him how to use it. A desk, a chair, a computer: what else? He was subletting the apartment on Ludlow Street to a friend of his brother's, leaving all the furniture behind, even the radio, TV and VCR. The only things he was taking up to Britta's was his typewriter, his books and papers, a trunk filled with clothing. He had been in the apartment for seven years but he wouldn't miss any of it.

Some new people, a couple, had moved upstairs about a year before and they liked to play music late at night, jazz mostly, so loud he could feel the ceiling vibrate. He could hear bedsprings creaking as they made love at five in the morning. He could hear them fighting, what sounded like plates smashing against the kitchen wall. The next day Richard invariably saw them in the street with their arms around each other as if nothing had happened. The man had a blonde ponytail and a beard and never acknowledged that Richard was his neighbor no matter how frequently they passed in the hallway. His companion, a small dark-haired woman with bright eyes and a mole under her lower lip, was more outgoing. Once they met at the mailboxes and she asked Richard if all the noise bothered him. She looked at him wide-eyed, apologetic, and Richard interpreted her gaze as a cry for help. At least that's what he wanted to believe. He tried to catch a glimpse of her neck under her sweater to see if she had any visible bruises. He wanted to think that she was asking him to help her escape her lover, but he couldn't be sure.

The anxiety attacks occurred without warning. Sometimes there was a specific reason: Britta would call Richard at the store or at his apartment and he wasn't there. She would hear his voice on the answering machine and feel like the slightest breeze could blow her away. Often, she would hang up without leaving a message. As far as she knew, he was dead, or with another lover. It was the uncertainty of it all that made her heart quiver; she raced to the bathroom to be alone with her imaginary fears. She wanted to throw up, but couldn't. She knelt in front of the toilet bowl until the pain in her chest subsided. She had lied enough to others in her own life to know how easy it was to deceive someone. She had no evidence that Richard was lying to her but she knew if she looked hard enough for a sign of betrayal she would find it somewhere. The man at the store, Richard's boss, hung up on her when she began questioning him.

She had the feeling that Richard was pretending not to be there in order to torture her. She never knew for certain whether the person she talked to would tell Richard she called. There was

53

no certainty he would get the message and call back. When she finally spoke to him, later, she would ask, in the calmest of voices, where he had been when she had called, and he would say, dead-pan: "I was on a break" or "I went for a walk." There was no way she could keep track of what he was doing every second of the day. He wasn't a dog, after all, with a leash and a collar, but maybe that's what she needed. She had a dog once, but it was killed in an accident. It had run into the street and was hit by a truck.

"Why don't you take the whole day off?" Deva said.

He had told his boss at the hardware store that he was quitting on Friday. There was no reason why he couldn't call him up today and tell him that he was never coming back. They would deduct some money from his last paycheck, but what did it matter? He went into Deva's bedroom, carrying the cup from Cancun, and dialed the number of the store. Deva followed him, draping her robe over the back of a chair. She sat down beside him on the bed and put her hand down the front of his pants. He wondered what Britta would think when she called him at work and his boss or one of his co-workers told her he had quit. Maybe she would change her mind and cancel the wedding?

MONEY UNDER THE TABLE

You can say I was holding out my hand to one of them. There were two of them with me in the room, one in a silk dress that resembled a short slip, the other in cutoffs and a Chinese blouse. It had been my suggestion to go to her room before I was too drunk to walk. The mother of one of them was somewhere behind the door. I could hear her rustling around outside and I knew it was just a matter of time before she would enter without knocking and turn on the light. The one with the slip was lying alongside me, playing with the buttons on my shirt, while the other was sitting on the edge of the bed. Except for my shoes, I was still fully dressed.

It was a novelty to be in an apartment on Park Avenue, the largesse of one room expanding into another. Closets as big as the rooms I lived in with my mother and sister in the Bronx. There were paintings on every wall, clusters of small ones or one large one, all of them in ornate frames, as well as vases with fresh flowers, a whole table of potted plants. In one painting, above a mantelpiece with another row of vases, a young blonde man on horseback was rescuing a woman wearing a white cape from the arms of a gray-haired man brandishing a whip. The woman was clinging to the man's waist, pressing her breasts against his back, her cape flying behind her like a wing. There was a spotted dog running alongside the horse, nipping at its heels.

In another painting, a teenage girl wearing horn-rimmed

glasses and a long Victorian dress with a high collar was sitting at a dining room table surrounded by plates of rotting fruit. A rat hovered on the edge of the table, waiting for the girl to turn her head so it could take a bite out of a rotten pear. The fruit and the plates made shadows on the white tablecloth. The girl wasn't shocked by the world of the painting in which she was the only human inhabitant. She stared straight ahead, her eyes bulging behind her thick lenses, but she obviously knew the rat was there. Her gaze was filled with the acceptance of a world where a rat had as much place at the dining room table as a person. Just because she wasn't going to eat the fruit didn't mean it had to go to waste.

I imagined secret hallways, tile bathrooms with gold faucets and monogrammed towels, guest rooms, a room for the *au pair* girl or the maid, storage rooms and rooms where people had died. My soul flew out of the top of my head as soon as I passed over the threshold; I felt like lighting a cigarette and stamping it out on the Persian rug. There was a lifetime of sadness hidden in the folds of the drapery that sealed off the apartment from the life in the street. I was grateful to my friends for inviting me into their world but the redundancy of possessions made me feel crazy. The rooms resembled tombs or caves, places to hide. It was possible for members of a family to live in an apartment like this for years and never see one another.

I assumed that the woman who opened the door for me was the "cook" or the "maid." She didn't look as if she had lost her sense of pride or was embarrassed by her color. Why should she? Her license to be here was her willingness to serve others. She studied me carefully, my face and clothing, to see whether I was worthy of the company of her employer's daughter. The door closed on my fingers and I bit my lips to fight back the pain. For a moment I wondered if I'd come to the right place. (It was the right place, but it wasn't "me" who was there.) The maid told me to wait; when she disappeared I unbuttoned my coat. It didn't sound like a party (when Linda called, earlier in the week, she had said "I'm having a

party Friday night — why don't you come over?"); in fact, I would-
n't be surprised if Linda's mother, or a surrogate mother, suddenly
appeared to inform me that her daughter was sick. It wasn't the
first time I'd traveled on the subway to Manhattan only to be disappointed by a last minute change of plans. No doubt the girl, Linda
or anyone, if this was the case, was standing behind a door at the far
end of the apartment, hand over mouth to muffle laughter. Getting
me to travel all the way to Manhattan from the Bronx was a way of
testing her power, the equivalent of tossing a dog a bone at the end
of a string and then withdrawing it until it was out of reach. Only
a few weeks ago, in the pouring rain, I traveled for an hour on the
subway to a new high-rise on the Upper East Side overlooking
Central Park only to be greeted at the door by the mother of the girl
I was going to see. "Amber's not home at the moment," the woman
said, "but I know she'll be happy to hear you stopped by." Only the
night before on the phone Amber had made me promise to arrive
any time after eight o'clock. Her parents were going to the theater;
we could be alone for a few hours. I was amazed how little effort
her mother put into lying in a convincing way. The least she could
do, I thought, was offer me a cup of hot chocolate before sending
me home in the rain, but as an accessory to an act of cruelty such
gestures weren't permitted. She aimed her gaze at a point directly
above my head and spoke without moving as if her jaw was wired
in place. It was the same remote tone she used when she talked to
one of her servants. What difference did it make to her whether I
believed her or not?

It wasn't unusual to make love to someone over the weekend
and ignore the person when you passed her in the hallway at
school a few days later. I saw Linda coming and looked the other
way. Once I had gone out of my way to meet her in front of her
locker or on the slope of the ball field behind the school. Now I left
school early, before her last class ended, going out the back
entrance and cutting across the parking lot to avoid meeting her.
When I arrived home there was a note in my mailbox — "I miss

you" — with her initial. Later that night my friend Harris called and asked me for details about my weekend and I told him everything, not realizing how jealous he could be, though I knew he was no longer a virgin and had numerous girlfriends of his own. I hadn't planned to mention Linda's name but he kept asking questions — "What's she like in bed?" — goading me on until I said something worth repeating. In this way, what people said about you determined your reputation, your popularity or lack of it. No one I knew went to church or believed in a religion that discouraged you from touching another person's body, though there were some who were less curious than others, who were too engrossed in their dutifulness towards schoolwork and getting into college to pay much attention, while still others — a few of us, anyway — were frightened of falling in love and getting hurt. I was in the latter category, though my curiosity was stronger than fear, and getting hurt (being rejected or spurned), I realized, once I'd experienced it a few times, was something I'd learn to survive. Someone older than I was told me that if I wanted to be a writer I had to experience everything, the whole spectrum of emotions that went along with being in love, but I never sought out pain that wasn't worth it in the end.

The two girls came out of nowhere and told me they were hungry. I only knew one of them, the one who had called me about the party. Apparently the other was her out-of-town cousin. That's how she introduced her. "We're hungry," they said, in unison, as if it were somehow in my power to provide food for them on the spot. I assumed if they were hungry they could always ask the maid or the cook to prepare something. I could hear a voice from another room in the apartment that was probably Linda's mother talking on the phone. The cousin was the one wearing the short silk dress. We were standing in the foyer, surrounded by more paintings and flowers. Linda's cousin brushed her wiry hair away from her face and showed me the stud in her ear. She had gone to MacDougal Street to get her ears pierced that afternoon. The jeweler had tried to put his hand between her legs and now she was frightened that her ear was infected. Both of them complained about how much they hated school. The one from out of town, who was taller than I was, said she had a crush on one of her teachers, her biology teacher, and that it was just a matter of time before they went to bed together. It was a common practice, in her town, for the teachers and students to sleep together. The teachers often called their students into their offices after class for "special conferences" and locked the doors. No one seemed to mind, the students least of all, though no doubt some of their parents would have complained it they knew.

We were sitting on the sofa in the living room smoking when the doorbell rang and Linda's mother appeared.

"It's her boyfriend," Linda said.

Her cousin, Devereaux, who had been yawning ever since I arrived, suddenly looked interested. "Is he cute?"

In fact, he was in his early seventies, and walked with a cane like a retired Russian count. Linda's mother led him across the threshold into the apartment, holding his arm and taking small steps to match his, but she didn't bring him into the living room to introduce him to her daughter or her friends. "What do you think they do together?" Devereaux asked. She slouched against the cushions at the end of the sofa, swinging her legs in my direction. I noticed that she was wearing a gold chain around one of her ankles and when I asked her about it she said that her boyfriend had given it to her. Apparently her boyfriend was much older than she was — "He's twenty-two" — and had just been expelled from the Naval Academy at Annapolis for cheating. "He didn't want to go into the Navy anyway," she said. Now he was back in the small town where she lived, hanging out in the local commons while he pondered his future. She had actually known him when she was much younger, when she was eight and he was fifteen and he used to deliver groceries to her house from the local supermarket. She remembered that she was often alone in the house when she was eight years old, especially between the hours of three-thirty and five-thirty, and that it was then that he usually came by with the groceries. Her mother often gave the people in the supermarket a list before she went to work since she had no time to go shopping herself and he would deliver the groceries in a shopping cart and carry the bags into the kitchen. Much later, when they had become lovers, she reminded him of their first encounters, but he scratched his head and claimed he didn't remember anything. "I delivered so many groceries to so many people, why would I remember you?" She would stand at the window waiting to see him coming down the street wheeling the cart filled with groceries. Then she would race to the door and stand there with a dollar bill in her hand (her mother had instructed her to give him the dollar after he finished the job) as he carried the bags into the kitchen. She had been tempted to offer to touch his penis (they could go down to the basement to do it) just to see what it looked like but she didn't have the nerve. Now she was thinking of dropping out of high school so they could travel around the country together. He had been offered a job in Chicago and had asked her to come along.

"You and your boyfriend can live here," Linda said. "I'm sure my mother wouldn't mind."

I was sitting on the sofa. Linda was kneeling at my feet with her arm on my knee. Devereaux was lying lengthwise across the couch with her feet on my lap. Linda and I had slept together earlier in the year but had ignored one another at school as if we were sorry it had ever happened. I had thought she was angry at me for never calling her and was surprised when she invited me to her party. I was going to ask whether anyone else was coming over but I didn't want to give the impression that I was bored with their company. On the contrary, I was flattered that I was the only guest. I lit a cigarette with a gold lighter and put my hand on Devereaux's leg. Her skin was white and smooth and she didn't push my hand away. It was then that I looked up and saw the painting of the young blonde man on horseback and the woman in the cape. The gray-haired man was standing with a whip in his hand. His arm was raised but it was a meaningless gesture. The woman, who was possibly his daughter, had already made her escape.

I always enjoyed traveling from the apartment in the Bronx where I shared a room with my older sister to the apartments of classmates who lived in Manhattan. Central Park West and Park Avenue were my favorite streets. If I had a choice, I guess I would have preferred a room with windows overlooking the park; if the apartment was high up, a view of the East River or the Hudson. I came from a world where anything that wasn't purely functional was considered a luxury, and where there was no value attached to an object that was beautiful for its own sake. I passed through the marble lobby of Linda's building as through a hall of mirrors, the potted trees and imitation Louis XIV chairs upholstered in burgundy, and smiled at the doorman when he asked "What apartment?" and called me "Sir." No doubt one of the girls had answered the intercom and assured the doorman that it was appropriate for me to come upstairs. But he eyed me suspiciously nonetheless, just in case the police questioned him later about a rape or a burglary. I wanted to assure him that I wasn't going to tie anyone up or ransack anyone's apartment, but it wasn't something I could put into words.

The doorman, who was in his mid-twenties, looked at me enviously as I headed towards the elevators. I sympathized with him as best I could. How could he feel anything but envy? I knew what it felt like to go to a party and meet someone I was attracted to who was obviously with someone else. I remember, at one party, going to the bedroom where I had put my coat and where two people I knew were fucking on the bed. They had swept all the coats onto the floor and were making love with the lights on. I don't think they knew I was in the room and if they did they wouldn't care. They wouldn't stop what they were doing because I had come in looking for my coat. It was probably on the floor, under the pile of other coats. The woman might even ask me to join them. She was on top of the man, her back facing me, as I entered the room. I remember how empty my own life felt at that moment, seeing the couple on the bed while I was about to go home alone, and how much I envied them, as no doubt the doorman envied me (wasn't he sick of his life, as well?) as I walked through the lobby.

I could imagine Linda teasing him (in the same way I had seen her flirting with her teachers at school), playing with the tassels on the shoulders of his uniform or leaning forward so he could see down the front of her blouse. "Let me try on your cap," she said, snatching it from the top of his head before he had a chance to stop her. She preened in front of the mirror, tilting her head from side to side. "I won't give it back to you," she said, holding the cap behind her, "until you kiss me." Sometimes she flitted through the lobby without even glancing at him. Other times she arrived at the building in a taxi and he helped her carry her packages to her apartment. On other occasions, she engaged him in long intimate conversations. "My period started today," she said to him as if she was reporting the evening news. She would talk, until her face was red and perspiring, about how much she hated her mother, how she wanted to kill her. As a joke, she offered him a thousand dollars to murder her mother. When he told her he had more important things to do than talk to her about her problems, she acted insulted and ignored him for days. She had lived her entire life among servants, maids, nannies, doormen, *au pair* girls and private tutors. She had bathed in their subservience. It was the privilege of people with money, or so she assumed, to treat the people who worked for them as they pleased.

It was almost midnight when I suggested we go to her room. We were drinking beer and listening to a record of Frank Sinatra singing "The House I Live In." I didn't drink much and after two or three beers I began nodding out. Linda said she had once met Frank Sinatra at a party. She was about to tell us the story when Devereaux swung her legs over the side of the couch and stood up.

"Well, let's go inside," she said, smoothing her dress over her thighs.

She had obviously heard the story of how Frank Sinatra had

attended a party at Linda's mother's house (it was Linda's mother's birthday and she had given herself a party), and how Linda — who was only five years old at the time — had sat on his knees while he sang "The House I Live In." (I guess there are some things you never forget.) Devereaux hated Frank Sinatra but knew better than to voice her opinion. There was a rumor that Linda was Frank Sinatra's daughter, but no one knew for sure. I followed them from the living room down a hallway into Linda's bedroom. It was the same room where we had made love earlier in the year. All the beer and the music was making me feel drowsy (it seemed like yesterday that I had been there) and I stretched out on Linda's king-sized bed and closed my eyes. I don't know how much time passed, probably only a minute or two, when I heard the sound of someone outside the door of the room. It was Linda's mother.

Devereaux was lying next to me on her side studying the lines in my hand. Linda was sitting at the end of the bed. I was thinking that I would reach out and pull her backwards in our direction when I heard the sound at the door, a kind of rustling. We were all in bed together, we were all fully dressed. Linda's mother opened the door of the bedroom and turned on the light. She gasped when she saw us and crossed her arms over her breasts. She had short silver hair, a wide face with a long pointy nose, and a blunt disapproving expression, like the warden in a woman's prison. We were the inmates and she had come to check on what we were doing.

"Can't we have *any* privacy," Linda said.

She spoke in an accent that reminded me of a movie actress playing the role of a spoiled southern belle, the daughter of a plantation owner, but I couldn't remember the name of the actress or the movie. Her mother made a noise in the back of her throat that sounded like a key turning in the lock of a prison cell or the rotted latch of an old trunk. It was the sound of moral superiority and hypocrisy, of growing old in the absence of desire and pleasure. She stood there for about thirty seconds like a dog lost in the rain, breathing heavily. Finally, she closed the door behind her but didn't turn out the overhead light.

The two girls couldn't contain themselves. They laughed loud enough so that Linda's mother, retreating down the hallway, could hear. "What would Frank think?" Linda asked. It was a private joke. She rolled around on the floor, pounding her fists into the carpet. Then she crossed the room to the mirror above her vanity and unfastened her blouse.

I had never been in bed with two women before. I had the feeling that they were both more experienced than I was (I'd been a non-virgin for two years and I could still name all the people I had slept with). They helped me undress, each of them tugging at the legs of my pants. Then Devereaux pulled me on top of her and we made love while Linda watched. She was thin and bony, flat-chested, with hips like a boy. Occasionally I reached out and touched Linda's breasts or put my hand between her legs so she didn't feel left out. The overhead light was still on and I could see every pore in the skin of the neck of the girl moving beneath me.

"You can come inside me if you want," Devereaux said. "I don't care."

And later: "I want your baby. I want to have a baby. Make me pregnant."

The first time Linda and I made love it had lasted only a few minutes. We were both half drunk and didn't even bother taking off our clothes. I knew that being "good in bed" was defined (at least from the man's point of view) by staying power and frequency. The best lovers were those who could do it four or five times in a single night. I wondered if I had the reputation, as a consequence of coming quickly when I was with Linda and then leaving immediately afterwards, of being an indifferent lover, someone who cared only for his own pleasure. I wondered whether Linda had told her friends about me. Truthfully, I had no real idea about how to give another person pleasure. I assumed that when a woman cried out it meant she was having an orgasm. I didn't know how to differentiate cries of pleasure that lead up to having an orgasm from the cries that accompanied the orgasm itself. I never made any noise when I made love, not even when I came. I think I was too conscious of what I was doing (at being "good") to really enjoy it.

"Harder," Devereaux kept saying and Linda, leaning over me like an animal trainer, repeated what she said just in case I didn't hear.

"Don't come yet," Linda instructed me. "I'm too sore to make love."

"You're sore from fucking the doorman," Devereaux said. "I heard you."

She turned her head to one side, not looking at me, and stared at her cousin defiantly.

"Shut up," Linda said. She toppled backwards as if struck by a blow.

I continued to push against her but I was just going through the motions. I felt like slapping Devereaux across the face just to see what she would say. I pretended that I was making love to Colleen McGrath, my English teacher, to keep myself interested: she was leaning over her desk in the deserted classroom and I was lifting her dress from behind. I decided that I didn't care about my reputation as a lover. Linda could tell her friends anything she wanted. I began moving rapidly. Devereaux wrapped her legs around my back and lifted her ass off the sheet.

"Have you ever made a baby before?" she hissed in my ear. "This is your first one, I bet. Do you want a boy or a girl?"

I was lying on top of her, still inside, my face buried in her neck. For a moment I couldn't remember her name.

"I feel like a dog," Linda said. "A sheepdog."

Someone was hammering against the bedroom door.

"Who is it?" Devereaux and Linda shouted in unison.

"Telephone for Devereaux. Long distance." It was a woman's voice, not Linda's mother, but the maid who had let me in.

"Get off me," Devereaux said, but I didn't move. "Linda, tell him to get off."

I was tempted to hold her down until she begged me to let her get up, until she started crying, until she began whining like a dog in a cage. She punched my arm and bit my shoulder but I grabbed her by the hair and pulled her away.

"I think she wants you to get up," Linda said.

As soon as Devereaux left the room Linda rolled towards me. She put a pack of Old Golds, a silver lighter and a glass ashtray on the sheet between us. She looked genuinely happy to have me all for herself. The first thing she did was apologize for what happened last year, for not calling me back after we slept together. I told her I was sorry as well for never responding to her note. She looked at me as if I was crazy (what note?) and I wondered if I was confusing her with someone else. I could visualize the note, the words "I Miss You" followed by the initial "L." I assumed that Linda had written it but I could have been wrong.

It was raining out and I told her that maybe I should begin thinking about going home and she suggested I spend the night. Her mother wouldn't like it but I could always sneak out before dawn. I asked her if she was really having an affair with the doorman.

"You'll tell everyone at school," she said.

"I won't," I promised, trying to reassure her, but I knew she had the right to feel concerned.

"You'll talk to Harris — he's your best friend, isn't he? — and he'll tell everyone."

She paused to crush her cigarette in the ashtray and light another.

"I'm so sick of all the kids at school. Some of them are such babies, especially the guys. I wanted to see what it was like with someone older. Lenny is twenty-six, he has two kids, he lives in Astoria. It isn't like we're going to run off together. He just comes up here, stays an hour. Sometimes we don't even take off our clothes." She blushed. "I love his uniform. I have to admit that's part of it. He even carries a gun in a holster strapped to his shoulder. Sometimes we stand at the window and point it at the people on the street. My mother's been traveling a lot recently and I'm alone here most of the time except for Juanita the maid and she won't tell anyone. Not about Lenny. She likes Lenny and knows that he'll lose his job if my mother finds out he's been here."

She propped a pillow under her head and stretched out on her back, blowing smoke rings at the ceiling.

"Devereaux's really beautiful isn't she? Every guy I introduce her to falls in love with her. I was so jealous of her when we were growing up."

Her hair was mostly brown with red highlights and fell in long waves over her forehead and shoulders. It was Linda's hair that had attracted me when I first saw her in the hallway at school. My friend Harris had pointed her out to me. When we were freshmen she sat in front of me in French so I had a whole year to study her hair. Even then, she was absent at least once a week and failed most of the tests. She always smiled at me when she stood up after class but I was too shy to talk to her.

"I'm going to nap for a few minutes. You have to promise that you're not going to leave."

Then a minute later:"I was in love with you last year. Did you know that? At least I thought I was. I had a crush on you even when I used to sit in front of you in French. I used to wear special clothing but you never even looked at me. I followed you around school. The only reason I took that class was because you were in it."

She was asleep now. It felt odd to be lying next to a naked woman and to feel no particular excitement or pleasure. Only two years ago I spent half my waking hours studying the pictures of naked women in magazines like *Playboy* and *Adam* and reading the sexy passages of novels like *The Amboy Dukes*, *A Stone For Danny Fisher*, *Battle Cry* and *The Hoods* until I knew them by heart. I reached out and put my hand on her thigh and she mur-

mured contentedly but didn't wake up. There was a rumor around school that she had an eating problem, that she went on binges where she ate nothing but chocolate for days and that's why her skin was so bad. Her face was white and puffy and was covered with tiny black dots. She was wearing too much make up: purple eye shadow and pink lipstick. I was beginning to feel like I didn't know Linda at all. I never realized how much she liked me when we were in French together and regretted that I missed my chance to go to bed with her then. Even when we finally did sleep together last year she had been more serious about me than I ever imagined. We had met at a party and she had asked me back to her apartment for a beer and we had ended up in bed. That was it. I guess I hurt her feelings by never calling back and by avoiding her at school. It was impossible, I realized, to know precisely what anyone was feeling at a particular moment. I didn't have enough experience to trust my instincts. It was rare for someone like Linda, who had no trouble finding boyfriends, to confess that she once had a crush on me and I wished I could reciprocate by telling her that I had loved her too. But all I remember feeling when we slept together was indifference. As soon as it ended I wanted to pull up my pants and leave.

I thought I heard voices in some other part of the apartment but I couldn't tell if it was Devereaux or Linda's mother and her boyfriend. I rolled over to the edge of the bed and walked naked to the window. Looking straight down, through the rain, I could see the doorman run out into the middle of Park Avenue to flag down a taxi. He didn't have a raincoat or an umbrella, only the cap that came with his uniform. I wondered if he and Linda made love in the bed where she was sleeping now or whether they went down to the basement where there was a mattress behind the boiler. It was my turn to feel envy. As doorman of a large building he had his pick of women to sleep with. He knew everyone's schedule, when a husband might be out of town, when it was convenient to suddenly appear at the door of someone's apartment. He had access to the intercoms of all the apartments in the building and could call up at any time to see if Linda was home. If she was interested in seeing him. "My mother's gone for the day, why don't you stop by?" Or: "I'm expecting a package. Why don't you bring it up?" No one minded if he was gone from his post for fifteen or twenty minutes, or even longer. He was always doing errands for the older people in the building. He had been working as the doorman of this particular building for five years. Before that, he had worked as an elevator operator in an office building on Wall Street. Everyone called him by his first name. "How's it going today, Lenny?" they said. At Christmas the tenants of the building pressed twenty dollar bills into his palm. He kept photographs in his wallet of his wife and daughters, to show off if anyone asked, as well as a picture of his ninety-year old grandmother who lived in Lithuania. It was common knowledge among the tenants in Linda's building that he was trying to save money so he could buy a house in New Jersey, in a town like Hackensack or East Orange. He told everyone in the building about the problem his grandmother was having getting a visa. He told them about the house in New Jersey. He showed them pictures. There was a rumor that his wife was pregnant again. Even Linda gave him a ten or a twenty dollar bill when he visited. She showed him the drawer where her mother kept her money. There was a gold bracelet on top of the bureau in Linda's mother's dressing room and he slipped it into his pocket before he left the apartment. Once he stole a twenty from Linda's wallet when she was asleep.

It was two in the morning. I had told my mother that I was planning to stay out later than usual. It was my habit to call her before midnight so she wouldn't worry that I had been mugged. I knew that she was lying in bed at that moment waiting for me to call. The last thing I wanted to do was put on my clothes and go looking for the telephone. I didn't want to get into the subway, which ran irregularly if at all this late at night, and return to my apartment in the Bronx. ("A ten minute walk from the Bronx Zoo,"

I said, when people asked me where I lived.) The last time I went home on the subway this late a tall black man in a tan trenchcoat asked me if I wanted to "mess around." I wasn't sure what he meant and I didn't ask. I had enough money to take a taxi but the idea of waking up in the bedroom in the Bronx with my sister sleeping in the bed across the room didn't appeal to me as much as waking up between Linda and Devereaux.

In a corner of the room there was a floor to ceiling bookcase containing magazines, stuffed animals, a radio and a portable record player. There was an entire shelf devoted to records. The first record I noticed was a boxed set of *Tristan und Isolde*. I remembered that after we made love a year ago Linda had asked me what kind of music I liked and I said "opera" though I only liked one opera, and when she asked me my favorite I said *Tristan und Isolde*. I wondered if she had bought the opera on my recommendation, in an attempt to impress me so that when we saw each other again we'd have something to talk about. I thumbed through the other records on her shelf but *Tristan und Isolde* was the only opera. Her taste in music, as far as I could tell from her record collection, tended towards show music like *Oklahoma*, *The King & I* and *West Side Story* and albums by popular singers like Frank Sinatra, Eddie Fisher and Nat King Cole.

I remember telling my friend Harris that I had spent the night with Linda. "She'll sleep with anyone," he had said, emphatically, as if I'd cheapened myself by going to bed with her. I was tempted to ask whether he had ever slept with her or if he had wanted to sleep with her and she had rejected him but by then he was telling me about his new girlfriend Margot. I held the receiver away from my ear and thought guiltily of how I had purposely avoided Linda at school. We had met at her locker in the basement every day leading up to the night we spent together. We had talked on the phone in the evening. She had asked me questions about her English homework — we were both reading *Sons and Lovers* — and I had tried to help her, but she had little confidence in her ability to learn anything. She had failed half her subjects the year before and was on probation. That day, in the mail, I had received a note with the words "I miss you" followed by her initial. After making love (in this room, in this bed) she had started crying. It wasn't the first time I had been with a woman who had burst into tears immediately after we made love. I asked Linda what was wrong and she said that she liked me a lot, more than she ever liked anyone, but she knew I didn't care about her at all. "I hate myself," she said. I put my arm around her shoulders to comfort her. "I like you a lot too," I told her, willing to say anything if she would only stop crying. "I really do."

As soon as she quieted down, I went to the bathroom and threw up. I washed my face in the sink with its gold faucets and inspected the medicine cabinet. The only prescription medicine was a jar of skin cream with Linda's name on it. Before leaving the apartment, I returned to her bedroom. She was lying on her stomach, as I'd left her, with her skirt hiked above her waist, I found a blanket which had fallen to the floor and covered her naked legs. She spread her legs slightly and lifted her head from the pillow and moaned. "I'm going now, Linda," I said, but she didn't respond.

My mother had a subscription to the Metropolitan Opera for her and my father but my father was sick so my mother asked if I wanted to go. I was twelve years old.

"It's in German," my mother said. "Sprechen Sie Deutsch?"

On the train downtown she told me what she knew about the story.

"It takes place on a ship," she said. "At least that's where it begins. Later, they go to a castle. Tristan is bringing Isolde to marry his Uncle Marke. It's a complicated story. Apparently Tristan murdered Isolde's former boyfriend. Isolde was planning to revenge her boyfriend's death by killing Tristan but they fell in love instead. Tristan was sick and she nursed him back to life. They just looked at each other and fell in love. I guess neither of them had ever seen anyone as beautiful as the other. Anyway, Tristan feels guilty about murdering her boyfriend. He won't admit to himself that he's in love with her so he offers her to his Uncle Marke. Isolde isn't happy with this arrangement. She loses her boyfriend, she falls in love with her boyfriend's murderer. Now she's being forced into a marriage with a person she never met. The last thing she wants to do is get married to Tristan's uncle. She complains to her maid Brangaene that she wants to kill herself. Brangaene has two magic potions, a death potion and a love potion. Just before the ship arrives at King Marke's castle, Tristan goes to Isolde's cabin. She's been insisting all the time that he come to see her but he's been trying to avoid her the whole trip. So he's there and the first thing he does is give her his sword. He hands it to her and orders her to kill him to revenge the murder of her boyfriend Morold. Instead she points to the cup with the magic potion and tells him to drink. She assumes it's the death potion. He drinks without hesitating and then she grabs the cup and drinks the rest. All this is taking place as King Marke and his entourage are gathering on the shore to meet the ship. All the sailors on the boat are going crazy. Both Tristan and Isolde assume they're about to die. In the last minutes before they're going to die they feel free to admit their love for one another. But they're not going to die. Brangaene poured the love potion into the cup instead. They can't believe that they're still alive...."

I thought she had finished, but that was only the end of Act One. It took almost an hour to get from our neighborhood in the Bronx to the area south of 34th street where the Met was located. I rarely went anywhere alone with either of my parents. I had reached the stage where I defined independence as doing things on my own or with my friends. I hoped that I didn't meet anyone I knew on the train or at the opera. My mother told me that I couldn't go unless I wore a jacket and a tie and I was tempted to tell her she could rip the ticket into tiny pieces for all I cared. She buttoned my shirt until it pinched the skin on my neck. She flattened the tie under the collar and held the wide and narrow ends in front of her. We were the same height now but I could remember when I came up to her waist and then her breasts. The tie had a pattern of play-ing cards against a gold field. It took her three tries before she tied it in a way that satisfied her.

"Maybe if you wore ties more often," she said, "you'd learn how to do this yourself."

The seats were in the second balcony, a few rows back, near the center. My mother kept exclaiming how perfect the seats were, and how expensive. She told me that when she was younger she and her friends would sit in the last row of the top balcony where it was impossible to see anything but where you could still hear per-fectly. My mother kept looking around to see what other people were wearing. We were a few minutes early and I sat back on my red cushioned seat and studied the program.

"A lot of people hate Wagner," my mother said. "He was Hitler's favorite composer."

The two seats to my right were empty. They were still empty as the lights began to dim and the conductor took his place on the podium, turned and bowed to the audience. There was a small lamp on the podium so he could follow the score. The orchestra had been warming up for some time, but after the applause for the con-ductor died down there was total silence. Behind me I heard the sound of human voices: apparently the usher was arguing with some latecomers. "It's started," he was saying. "You can't go in." There was a commotion in the aisle. Then a man and a woman made their way down the steps to the row where I was sitting. A man behind me remarked about how inconsiderate some people were. The lights were fading but I caught a glimpse of the woman. She was wearing a conservative gray and black striped dress, black stockings and high heels. The man who was with her was much older and had a white goatee. Both of them were carrying their coats over their arms. As the woman sat down she brushed my hand with her elbow, we were both vying for the arm rest between our seats, and pressed her face close to mine, close enough so I could smell her lilac perfume, and whispered: "I'm sorry." She settled back in her seat with her coat on her lap just as the overture began.

I tried to concentrate on what was happening on the stage but I couldn't resist glancing at the woman about once a minute. (On the train ride downtown, my mother told me that my father often fell asleep before the first act was over.) The stage was still very dark. There was the vague outline of a ship painted on the far wall. Sailors were lying around near the mast in the center of the deck. It was an old-fashioned wooden ship with a wide curve in the middle. The sailors were apparently just waking up or had been awake most of the night. There was a man standing alone, looking out to sea. I assumed that was Tristan. Another man with long curly hair was lying at his feet like a huge dog. There was another area of the stage that resembled a tent at the far end of the ship with a ladder leading from the tent to the deck below. This was Isolde's tent, or so it seemed. She was lying on a couch, her face buried in the cushions. Her maid was looking wistfully over the side of the ship. The wall of the stage was painted two shades of blue to distinguish the sky from the water. It was either dawn or late evening. The woman next to me stared directly in front of her, but once when I glanced over she tilted her head towards me and smiled. She was sitting closer to me than she was to the man with the goatee who might have been her father or uncle or an older brother. I shifted towards her in my seat (it was just a matter of inches, of fractions of inches), so that eventually I was sitting closer to her than I was to my mother.

I realized that it wasn't necessary to know the story. What was important was to get caught up in the immensity of it all. The characters in the opera were speaking to each other, but instead of talking they were singing. There was often nothing particularly dramatic about what they were saying. The singing made it seem more dramatic than it was, only because the voices sounded so beautiful set to music. I began to listen more closely, despite myself, in an attempt to understand what made opera so interesting to so many people. Also, I wanted to impress the woman sitting next to me with my devotion to the music. I even forgot about her for a few minutes, then I felt the toe of her shoe brushing my leg. I looked over and she was staring at the stage through a pair of opera glasses. Without saying a word, she offered them to me, as if she assumed (because of our proximity) I had as much right to use them as she. I think she was in her early twenties but she might have been a few years younger. Isolde and Brangaene were on stage. Isolde was wearing a long white dress which trailed behind her when she moved. Her hair was loose but not very long. She wore a complicated series of necklaces, gold and amber and lapis, which dangled almost to her waist. Her dress was very tight, especially around the breasts, and I wondered how she could breathe. She looked older than Tristan. More like his mother than a potential lover. She had a wild concentrated look in her eyes as if her mind was a tunnel with no light at the end and she gestured with both her hands as if she were gathering the words from the sky and then offering them back to the air itself in return for nothing. "They're talking about the potion," the woman next to me said. She put her hand on my arm. I felt like the drama had moved from the stage up into the balcony and that it was just a matter of time before everyone in the audience had their binoculars trained on us. Didn't she know that I was only twelve years old? Some people told me I looked older — fourteen or fifteen — but to my mind, when I stared at myself in the mirror, I looked like a child.

The man sitting on the other side of the woman was breathing heavily, occasionally taking a handkerchief from his jacket pocket and spitting into it, careful not to make any noise that might disturb the people behind us. "Here," I whispered, returning the opera glasses. The man behind me cleared his throat: we were disturbing his concentration. Once, on the bus ride home from school, I reached out and put my hand on the leg of a girl who was standing in the aisle near my seat, but she didn't tell me to take my hand away or cry out that she was being molested. I had seen her every day on the trip home and I had been trying to get the nerve to touch her. I tried to catch a glimpse of her face when I put my hand on her leg but her head was turned away. The bus was crowded: I was sitting down, she was standing next to me in the aisle. It occurred to me that I should offer her my seat but instead I reached out and put my hand on her leg. First I just grazed the skin with my fingers. She was wearing a gray skirt, knee-length, and carried her schoolbooks against her chest. Once my mother told me that a girl in the neighborhood, someone I knew, had been raped on the way home from school. My idea of rape had nothing to do with sex. It simply meant that someone had taken away her clothing and she was forced to walk home alone. I had an image of a naked girl wandering the winter streets. As Tristan and Isolde were vowing their undying love for one another (they had just sipped from the cup with the magic potion), I was sitting in the dark wondering if I should put my hand on the woman's leg.

At the end of Act One everyone stood up and applauded. The singers came out from behind the curtains and took their bows. The man with the goatee whispered something to the woman. With the lights on she looked older, maybe in her mid or late thirties. The man patted the breast pocket of his jacket to indicate that he wanted to smoke. It was a gesture my father made every night after dinner. My mother didn't like him to smoke in the kitchen so after dinner he left the table and sat in the living room with a cigarette and a cup of coffee and the newspaper. But first he patted his shirt pocket where he kept his cigarettes as the man with the goatee had done. The woman nodded her head in response to what he had whispered. They started towards the aisle, leaving their coats on their seats. My mother, whom I'd almost forgotten about, asked me if I wanted to get up and stretch.

I assume she was proud of me because I hadn't fallen asleep. The opera had started at seven and it was already eight-thirty and there were two more acts to go, it wasn't even half over. All about us people were talking, humming the music, comparing notes on previous performances which they had seen in Vienna or Milan. We were standing in the lobby and most of the people were smoking. Some of them talked in heavy accents. Some of them were talking about subjects that had nothing to do with the opera. I saw the woman talking with the man with the goatee. She was leaning against him as if she was having difficulty keeping her balance. She was drinking something out of a long-stemmed wineglass and holding the man's arm as he puffed cigarette smoke towards the ceiling. The heels of her shoes were pointed and very thin and maybe that was why she had trouble standing on her own. My mother always complained that she had difficulty walking when she wore new shoes. She said she hated to wear high heels but that they made her legs look more shapely. The woman who was sitting next to me was as tall as the man with the goatee. Her black hair fell like a dark cloud around her shoulders and along the sides of her face. We were standing a few yards away but I couldn't hear what they were saying. There were other women in black dresses with bare shoulders who were clinging to the arms of men in black pin-striped suits. My mother asked what I thought of the opera and I said that I wished it was in English so I could understand all the words but that otherwise I liked it quite a bit, especially the voices of the singers, especially Tristan. "He looks like a movie star," my mother said, "doesn't he?" There was the sound of a bell ringing in the distance and my mother said that was a signal to return to our seats. The people began putting out their cigarettes in the standing ashtrays but the man with the goatee and his tall girlfriend didn't move.

We made contact again during the second and third acts but not as often as before. There was almost no action in Act II except at the end. Most of the time Tristan and Isolde were standing on the stage singing to one another. I put my elbow on the arm rest and she leaned her arm next to mine. She turned her body in my direction and crossed her legs. I felt the toe of her shoe rubbing against my leg. It occurred to me that possibly such contact was normal.

We were sitting so close together it was impossible not to touch one another, if only accidentally. I had the feeling, as Act II stretched on into a kind of infinity of unrequited longing and despair, that if I put my hand under her dress she wouldn't mind. (My friend Harris had a theory that if you didn't act aggressively when you were with a woman, she assumed that you didn't like her.) At one point she tilted her head towards me and I thought she was going to rest her head on my shoulder. I was beginning to feel drowsy and I had to fight from dozing off. Occasionally the audience burst into spontaneous applause and I stared at the stage to see what I had missed but nothing was happening. All my attention was centered on the woman sitting beside me. I had the feeling that she would lose interest in me if I fell asleep. I had the fantasy of meeting her again, when I was older, how we would talk about the night we first met at the opera. "I kept wanting you to touch me," she said. "I thought I was going crazy." Her long dress, her black stockings, her high heel shoes ("stiletto" heels, as they were called), her black opal earrings, the sweep of her black hair as she shifted towards me in the dark. My mind began to wander. Someone on the stage was shouting and the voices of the singers had become louder and shriller, almost hysterical. It was a Friday night, at least I could sleep late the next morning. I had planned to go to the local movie theater, the RKO Pelham on White Plains Road, with my friend Harris. We often went on Saturday afternoon when the theater was crowded with people from the neighborhood, mostly kids our age or older. In every row there was a couple necking, oblivious to the movie or the people around them. Once I saw my sister, who was three years older than I, sitting in the back row of the balcony with a young black man. They were necking and the man had his hand down the front of my sister's blouse. Later, I saw my sister outside the theater. She was holding hands with the black man and told me if I ever told my parents what I had seen she would decapitate me, that was the word she used. I knew that it was just a matter of time before Harris and I went to the movies with the intention of picking up girls. (I envied the aggressiveness of the young man in front of me, only a few years older than I, who without thinking twice rested his hand on the front of the blouse of the girl sitting beside him.) Now Harris and I divided our time staring at the heads of the couples necking and the Biblical epic on the screen. Harris, even more than I, was preoccupied with the girls in our class at school. He had magazines with photographs of naked women hidden beneath the copies of *Sports Illustrated* under his bed. The theater smelled of hair tonic, eau de cologne, disinfectant. A halo of cigarette smoke (smoking was permitted in the balcony) blossomed in the air above the orchestra, slowly descending in an ever-expanding cloud above the embracing couples. Ushers patrolling the aisles directed their flashlights in the faces of anyone who was smoking or (sadistically) in the faces of the couples who were making out. There was a candy store next to the theater that had been closed by the police for selling pornographic comic books. That's where Harris and I were going to meet, at 2 P.M. I tried to imagine telling him about the woman at the opera but I knew he would never believe me.

My mother opened her pocketbook and took out a wad of tissues and pressed them to the side of her face. It was the third act and everyone was dying. Tristan was lying on a small sofa in the center of the stage. His servant, Kurvenal, had just killed Melot, Tristan's false friend. The woman next to me leaned towards the stage, holding her face in her hands, as if it were too painful to look. It was obvious, even to me, that Tristan was dying, that they were all going to die. But Isolde was still singing and the music was rolling over the sound of her voice like an immense wave and I knew that we had been sitting in the darkness for hours waiting for this moment. It was only at the very end that the words and music suddenly came together. It was almost as if Wagner had been teasing us up to this point, holding back, developing a theme and then cutting it short. Now the melody seemed to last forever, withdrawing into itself until it reached the boundaries of infinity. All the waves in the ocean were pouring over Isolde's outstretched arms. She was melting into the meaning of the words, clinging to each syllable. She was giving new meaning to the words with the sound of her voice. "Soon I'll be with you," she was singing, addressing Tristan's soul. They had planned to die together at the end of Act I but had sipped from the love potion instead. The music was like a ladder to heaven which they were climbing, step by step. Then the woman sitting beside me and my mother and the man with the goatee were on their feet. Everyone was applauding, tossing hats and flowers onto the stage. People were shouting and stamping their feet like young children. The woman next to me was crying too, wiping her eyes with a handkerchief which she had borrowed from her friend. The man with the goatee was standing on his seat shouting "Bravo!" The singers who played the roles of Tristan and Isolde were taking their final bows in the center of the stage. The singer who played Tristan gathered some of the flowers that had been thrown from the balcony and presented them to the singer who played Isolde. The woman next to me tilted her head in my direction, biting her lips as if she wanted to say something. I leaned towards her, the sleeve of my jacket touching her arm. It was pointless to say "Good-bye" when we had never really met. I felt like saying "I want to see you again" but I didn't have the nerve. I felt like embracing her, in the spirit of the moment, as Tristan and Isolde had embraced at the end of Act One. I had an image of her floating in the air above the orchestra. Self-contained, like an angel with blue hair. In another image, I saw her sitting on the side of an unmade bed in a hotel room. "It's unusual to find someone your age," she was saying, "who loves opera as much as you do." Her dress was pulled up to her waist and she was peeling her black stockings from her long legs.

I wondered if my mother was crying because of the opera or because she was thinking of my father, all the nights they had taken the subway downtown together to see a play on Broadway or to a concert at Carnegie Hall. Maybe she realized that they would never go to these places again. They had met twenty years before at a singles weekend in a hotel in the Poconos. At the time, they were both in their mid-thirties, and each of them had been married once before. My father was working as a letter carrier for the post office. Later, at my mother's insistence, he went back to school, and when he graduated with a degree in engineering he found a job as a city housing inspector. His job was to meet with landlords and housing contractors and check that they were maintaining proper standards in the buildings which they owned or were renovating. Often, contractors and landlords used the cheapest materials for their buildings. After a few years the pipes eroded and the wooden floors rotted away and tenants ended up suffering because the landlords tried to raise the rent so they could pay the cost of maintaining a building that was barely livable.

He would inspect buildings with people living in them where previous violations had been cited. Sometimes, when the violations were serious and the landlords and contractors didn't want to spend the money, they offered my father a bribe if he promised not to report them. They would hand him an envelope containing a hundred dollar bill, sometimes more than one. Maybe it was as simple as repairing a staircase or plastering a leaky ceiling. The landlords tried to get away with doing as little as possible. There were enough contractors who committed violations who didn't offer bribes to avoid suspicion when he accepted the bribes of the contractors who did. You could never be too careful. Some of the contractors gave him money every month. They would leave the money in a locker in Grand Central Station for which my father had the key. Every month he went to the locker and took out a white envelope filled with cash.

He spent his days driving around in a city-owned car, a Buick. Once I went with him on his rounds and he introduced me to some of the landlords and contractors. They had sagging jaws and stomachs, just like my father, and their skin was mottled from too much drinking. They called me "Albie's boy" and said I looked just like my old man, though I knew this wasn't true and that they were just saying it to please my father. I saw the white envelope pass from the pocket of one of the landlords to the breast pocket of my father's jacket. I saw the walls of corroded tenements, I climbed the urine-soaked staircases. While my father conferred with a man in a yellow hat, I stood in the rain and watched a tractor excavate some old stones. "It's not a bad job," he said, as we drove back to the Bronx. I sensed that he wanted some kind of confirmation that what he was doing was worthwhile, that I understood why he took the money, that it wasn't a crime, but I didn't give it. Every minute or so he patted the breast pocket of his jacket. *That* was his confirmation. I was just along for the ride.

My father kept all the money in our apartment. If he put any of it in the bank he would have to report it to the government and he didn't want anyone to ask him questions about where it came from. His bank account was regularly audited by the city to discourage him from taking bribes. The only people who knew he had this money were the members of our immediate family. The only way I knew about it was because I overheard my mother and father talking. Apparently, all her sisters and brothers wanted to borrow the money from him for one business venture or another and he refused to lend them a penny. Once, in the back of my father's closet, when Harris and I were playing, I found a shoebox containing a stack of hundred dollar bills. I made Harris promise never to tell anyone about the money but I always worried that he would tell his parents and that his parents would inform the police and that my father would lose his job and end up in jail.

We lived in a three and a half room apartment in the Bronx, a ten minute walk from the zoo. My sister and I shared a room. My father and mother slept in a bed in the living room. With all the money my father hid away, we could have moved at any time. But he was frightened that the housing commission would question where the money came from if he ever bought a house in the country or a new car. He had friends who had been investigated for withdrawing too much money at one time from their bank accounts. Any sudden transaction aroused the suspicions of the investigators. If he bought anything that cost a lot of money they would question him immediately. How could he afford a house in the country on his salary?

I asked my sister how much money she thought we had and she said that we probably had a hundred thousand at least. She was mad at my parents for never buying anything. What she wanted most of all was an apartment with a room of her own. She was sick of sharing a room with her brother. Who could blame her? When she was younger I used to watch her get dressed when she thought I was asleep. Now she put on a bathrobe, collected her clothing, and dressed in the bathroom. She wanted to live in an apartment where she could invite her friends over without feeling embarrassed. She had lost her virginity a few months before, or so I learned from reading her diary. She thought it was wrong for my father to take bribes. What difference did it make since we lived like paupers anyway?

My mother asked me what I wanted for Christmas. I surprised her by requesting a recording of *Tristan und Isolde*. She didn't realize that the opera had made such a big impression on me. She had cancelled her subscription to the Met because my father wasn't well enough to accompany her and she assumed that my sister and I weren't interested. My feelings about the opera were inseparable from my thoughts about the woman who had been sitting beside me. I masturbated daily, imagining her in different settings and in different poses. We were in a hotel room and she was lifting her dress over her head or we were in the last row of the balcony at the local movie theater and I put my hand down the front of her blouse. Listening to the opera was a way of reviving her image, of reliving the moment. I wanted my life to be like the explosion at the end of the opera when Tristan died and Isolde extended her arms towards heaven as the world crashed around her. The music accompanying her final song was what I imagined heaven was like, a continuous orgasm, building up and then exploding but never really subsiding. My sister was particularly impressed with me for requesting a record of an opera for Christmas and told all her friends that her brother was interested in classical music. She had one friend who played the piano and studied voice. When my sister told Jennifer that I liked *Tristan und Isolde* she clapped her hands (or so my sister informed me) and said that it was her favorite opera too.

My father's stomach problems grew worse. The word "cancer" was never mentioned, but what else could it be? I guess they thought I was too young to deal with the truth. Twice a week he went to the hospital for treatment. Often, when I said "Good night" or "Good morning" to him he stared at me from the bed in the living room as if I was a total stranger. The only person he enjoyed talking to was my sister Liddy. She sat on the side of his bed and read the newspaper aloud to him and told him about the courses she was taking in school and what her teachers were like. Sometimes she sang him one of his favorite songs, "I'm Walking Behind You," which Eddie Fisher had popularized a few years before, or "Hey There," in a voice that sounded like a scratchy record. She had perfected the technique of talking without demanding a response. She took it for granted that what she talked about was interesting to him, that it was more important to say anything than sit in morbid silence staring into space. When he didn't feel like talking he would communicate to her by writing notes. The fact that he preferred my sister's company over ours was obvious to my mother and I but neither of us minded. It was one less burden off my shoulders was the way I saw it. The only thing I could think of talking about with my father was sports. He liked to watch the Friday night boxing matches and I would join him in the living room, prop his pillows behind his back and adjust the antennae so the picture was clear, but I don't think he cared whether I was in the room with him or not.

He was on an extended leave of absence from his job. It occurred to me that if he quit his job he would be able to spend all his money and no one would question where it came from. Sometimes all he could eat for days was chicken broth which he drank through a straw. There was always a pot of broth warming on the stove. He had lost thirty pounds in the last year and I had to admit that he looked more handsome now that he was thinner. He had weighed over two hundred and twenty pounds before he became sick. I guess he assumed that the one thing he could spend his secret money on was food. He liked Chinese and Italian food, especially, but he hated going to restaurants. He would call up the restaurants in the neighborhood and they would deliver the food. The exception was a dairy restaurant on 2nd Avenue in Manhattan called Ratners that he liked to go to on Sundays. When he was well, we would all take the subway downtown to Orchard Street on Sunday afternoons to go shopping and afterwards we would eat at Ratners. There were two Ratners, one on 2nd Avenue and one on Delancy street. My father preferred the restaurant on 2nd Avenue. He knew the waiters there and always overtipped. On the subway uptown my mother scolded him for giving the waiters so much money. "The last of the big time spenders," she would say, though it was anything but true. I remember there were big baskets of bread and rolls on the table and my father ate practically half of them before the actual meal arrived. He would order mushroom barley soup and potato pancakes or cheese blintzes with sour cream. For dessert he had a bowl of fruit, nuts and raisins.

One afternoon I met my sister and her friends on the street and she introduced me to Jennifer, the girl who loved opera. She was a tall, awkward-looking girl with high cheekbones and a mass of unruly knotted reddish-brown hair which looked like it hadn't been washed in weeks. Not the type of girl I was attracted to, or who normally invaded my fantasy life. She was wearing an over-sized car coat with a hood so there was no way of knowing what her body was like. As far as Harris and I were concerned, and even though we knew that a girl's "personality" was important, the size of a girl's breasts was all that really mattered. Unlike my sister and her other friends, Jennifer wore neither make up or jewelry, none that was visible anyway.

"I've heard a lot about you," she said, and I averted my eyes, trying not to blush, while my sister and her friends laughed.

"They're a perfect match," one of them said.

A few days later, a Saturday when my parents were at the hospital and Liddy was at the movies with one of her boyfriends and I was lying on my bed reading *79 Park Avenue* by Harold Robbins which I had found in the back of my sister's bookcase, the phone rang and a woman's voice asked to speak to my sister.

"It's Jennifer," she said. "Remember me? We met on the street."

When I told her that Liddy wasn't home she paused for a moment as if she was saying a prayer for the dead and then asked if she could stop by anyway. She wanted to hear my recording of *Tristan und Isolde*, if I had the time to play it for her.

"I was really calling to see you," she said. "Are you alone?"

She was over in fifteen minutes. I helped her off with her coat and hung it in the closet while she sat on a chair in the small foyer and unfastened the snaps on her boots. It was snowing out but she wasn't wearing a hat and the tips of her hair glistened with melting crystals. She was wearing a black turtleneck and a red and black striped skirt with a big safety pin holding it together, black tights and a necklace of small bones. I guess I was supposed to ask her where she bought the necklace but I didn't want to be obvious, to be like everyone else. If my interest in opera set me apart from others then I had to act different in every way, or pretend to. All I wanted to do, from the moment she entered the apartment, was put my arms around her and bury my head between her breasts. I led her to the bedroom which I shared with my sister and she told me I should put on the last act of the opera. She stood very close to me, studying the record jacket, as I brushed the dust from the needle. My hands were trembling. Her hair, straighter and cleaner than it had been when I first saw her, hung over the sides of her face and alighted on her shoulders like wings.

I had to admit, as we stood there listening to the music, that I was thinking of the woman who sat next to me in the opera house. Whenever I looked at Jennifer I saw the woman's face. It was the moment when the lights in the opera house came on at the end of Act III and her eyes were swollen with tears. Yet she was smiling at me as a way of acknowledging what had passed between us in the dark. Nothing much had happened; but the fact that anything had happened was a kind of miracle.

I thought of my parents. The last thing I wanted was for them to return home suddenly and find me with my sister's friend. They'd been gone a few hours already and there was some talk that my father would have to stay overnight at the hospital so the doctors could do some tests. I had asked my mother when she was going to come home. She had hung her head and muttered, "I don't know," which of course she didn't. It was out of her control. These days she rarely gave me a specific answer to anything. If he was going to stay overnight at the hospital she would stay with him during dinner and until visiting hours were over. If he wasn't going to stay then they would come home together. But possibly they would wait until the snow let up. They might be forced to stay at the hospital if the storm became much worse. The night before I went into the kitchen at 2 A.M. for a glass of water and saw my mother sitting at the table with her head in her hands. My parents never discussed my father's illness with me but I was beginning to get the impression that they had given up hope.

Jennifer sat down on the side of my bed and beckoned me to join her. She told me that her parents were separated and that her father lived on MacDougal Street while her mother still lived in the Bronx and that she spent her weekends with her father but that this weekend he was out of town, he was a jazz pianist and sometimes he went on the road for a week or two with his band. So it was just by luck that she was in the Bronx today and she thought of calling my sister Liddy but realized that she really wanted to see me (it was her turn to blush). "If Liddy answered the phone," she said, "I was going to hang up." She said that her parents had taken her to see *Tristan und Isolde* when she was ten and that it had made a lasting impression on her. She began voice training lessons at the neighborhood music school and wondered if she'd ever be good enough to sing at the Met. She tried to learn some popular songs by listening to the radio, and to her father's records, but when she fantasized she was always in the center of the stage of a huge opera house in Italy or France, engulfed by waves of applause and adoration. She said that the reason her parents split up was because her father didn't make enough money as a musician and her mother wanted him to quit playing music and get what she called "a real job." She said she preferred going downtown on weekends and being with her father, that she wished she could live with him all the time, that her mother had a boyfriend who stayed over twice a week while she was there (and probably on weekends as well). He was a foreman for the sanitation department and left the apartment at about four in the morning to go to work. He had massive hands and a thick mustache and ate enormous platefuls of beef and chicken. He was always knocking on the bathroom door when she was taking a shower and asking if he could come in and pee. There was no lock on the bathroom door and she was frightened he was going to come in and rape her when he was drunk. Her mother kept saying that no one wanted to be a sanitation worker but the people who did the dirty work in life made the most money. Her mother wanted a lot of money, though she wasn't always this way. At one point in their life together she had encouraged Jennifer's father to pursue his career as a musician. They went to concerts and nightclubs and parties almost every night. It was when they moved to the Bronx, a few years after Jennifer was born, that things began to change. Maybe if they had stayed in Manhattan their lives would have been different. Now Jennifer's father had to ride the subway an hour each way to go to work, when he had work, playing in nightclubs in midtown or the Village. Sometimes he wouldn't return home till four or five in the morning. They didn't have enough money to hire a baby-sitter so Jennifer's mother could go with him, like in the old days. Her mother had wanted to be a painter but she had no confidence in herself. She felt about painting the way Jennifer herself felt about singing, that she was good up to a point. She couldn't decide whether she wanted to devote her whole life to singing any more than her mother could or couldn't decide whether to devote her energies to being a painter. It was after Jennifer was born and they moved to the Bronx that her mother began losing interest in both music and painting. She became obsessed with clothing, with her body, she went on a diet and lost so much weight all her old clothing no longer fit. And of course there wasn't enough money to buy a new wardrobe. She had an old sewing machine and began making clothing for herself. That's how she spent her days when her daughter was in nursery school and her husband slept. That's what she did when her husband was out all night at his job. They no longer slept together so she assumed he had girlfriends as well but after awhile she ceased to care. She had a dream of becoming a clothing designer or at least opening her own store. She began making clothing — dresses and skirts — and selling them to her friends. Eventually, as her reputation in the neighborhood grew, people she didn't know began calling her up and giving her work. But she could never save enough money to open her own business. There were weeks when Jennifer's father was out of work and all they had to support them was the money she earned making clothes. She tried to encourage her husband to find a job with a regular income so she could save some money but he refused to give up playing music. If he worked during the day he couldn't play his music at night. He couldn't go out of town if he was asked. Jennifer's mother wanted money so she could move out of the Bronx and open her own store. Her dream was to live in the suburbs, Westchester or Nyack. The sanitation worker boyfriend was a ticket out of the Bronx.

"I used to hear my parents fighting all the time," Jennifer said.

"It was like being in hell. Our apartment wasn't large and I think my father hit my mother a few times, they would throw plates at one another and frying pans until the neighbors complained. I knew my father was hitting her when my mother shrieked loudest — there was always a point in their fight when this happened. It was like her voice stopped sounding human, more like an animal when it's been stepped on. Once one of the neighbors called the police. I tired to cover my head with my pillow but it didn't help. Usually, after all the noise subsided, my father would look in on me and sit down on the side of my bed and wipe the sweat from my forehead. I was always recovering from a fever of some kind. I had fantasies of killing myself, which I could never tell anyone, about strangling myself with the telephone cord, taking fifty aspirins, slitting my wrists. I actually saw a movie with my friends where a woman kills herself in the bathtub by slitting her wrists with a razor and the water turns red. I wanted to do something that would wake my parents up but the only thing I could think of doing" — she lowered her voice, as if someone was listening — "was committing suicide."

There was death in the air, in her words and in the opera where Tristan was dying. The difference between art and life was that you could always start the opera from the beginning. You could turn back to page one, when the characters in the book were still alive. But when people die all that remains are memories, as meaningless as ashes in an urn. I tried to speed up the tape of my life and imagine what it was like to be fatherless. It occurred to me that I had been living with my father's absence for a long time, and that dying was just another version of not being there. Most of the time I tried not to think about dying. When I did, usually late at night lying in bed, I would rush to the bathroom and stare at myself in the mirror. The idea of not being was frightening to me. The cold porcelain against my skin as I leaned over the sink reassured me that I was alive at that moment. I made a vow to live my life as if any moment might be my last. To sleep no more than two or three hours a night, since sleeping was like being dead. I was shocked at the idea of suicide. For a moment, as she uttered the words "committing suicide," my desire for Jennifer vanished. The last thing I wanted was the idea of dying to intrude on my thoughts. Jennifer was like a character in a movie who had stepped off the screen into my arms. I wanted to fall in love with her in the moment of our being alone together but her words got in the way.

We stood at the window watching the snow blanket the parkway below. The cars were moving very slowly in the half-blizzard and I knew it would be a long time before my parents would ever return home. There would certainly be no point for my father to travel in this weather. Maybe my mother would come home later in a cab if the blizzard stopped.

"It's so beautiful, isn't it?" Jennifer said.

I didn't know whether she was talking about the opera or the snow.

"It's unusual for someone as young as you are" — the words stung for a moment — "to appreciate beautiful music."

I wanted to admit to her that I wasn't listening to the music, that whenever I played the opera I thought of the woman who had been sitting beside me in the opera house. By now I couldn't even remember her face. The man with the goatee was a stranger who had hired her to accompany him to the opera. She went with him to the opera once a week. On other nights she accompanied other men to dinner parties or the ballet. Sometimes she returned with them to their hotel rooms or apartments. They always paid her in advance. She was only nineteen years old but she looked older, mid-twenties at least. The man with the goatee liked her to take off her clothes and sit in a chair facing the bed until he fell asleep. Then she would join him in bed and fall asleep beside him. He never touched her.

Jennifer reached out and drew a heart in the frost on the windowpane.

"A cold heart," she said, and we turned to face one another.

Money Under The Table

"Don't you want to kiss me?" She was a few inches taller than I was and I had to raise my head so our lips could meet. Her mouth was open but as our faces collided she pulled away.

"Don't bite," she reprimanded me, in a way that reminded me of my mother. "Didn't anyone ever teach you how to kiss?"

She extended her tongue and touched the corners of my mouth, my lips, darted her tongue between my teeth. I tried to follow her movements as if we were dancing. For a moment just the tips of our tongues were touching. She took my tongue between her teeth. But it didn't hurt. She closed her eyes and darted her tongue in and out of my mouth. "This is called tongue-fucking," she said. She reached for my hand and as we stood at the window with the snow falling she guided it under her skirt. We came up for air but she continued kissing the side of my face, my neck. Then our mouths connected again and she grabbed my arm to keep from falling. Her breasts, I noticed, were larger than my sister's. She unbuttoned my shirt, kneeling slightly, so she could kiss my shoulders and chest. I remembered all the couples I had seen in the movie theater on Saturday afternoons, how it seemed like they could go on kissing one another for hours without stopping. The only time I ever kissed anyone before was during kissing games at parties, spin the bottle or post office. I'd never done it with my mouth open.

"Wait a minute."

She pulled away from me and took my hand and led me towards the bed which suddenly seemed too narrow for both of our bodies. Her skirt with the immense silver safety pin settled over her thighs.

"Did your sister tell you anything about me?" she asked.

"She said that you liked opera. That's all. That your favorite opera was *Tristan*."

"What do you think she'd do if she knew I came to visit you? I'm three years older than you, at least. What would anyone think? If I put on a lot of make up I can pass for twenty. Most of my friends

92

are older than I am. I wish Liddy liked me more but I understand why she doesn't. For a while we were both going out with the same guy and one time, at a party, he made love to both of us. First he took Liddy into one of the bedrooms, then me. Afterwards he took me home and left your sister at the party. Ever since then I have the feeling she hates me."

I was frightened that it was going to end here, that the words were going to take over. I was suddenly aware of the faces on the wall above my bed, a collage of magazine photographs of baseball players and movie stars. I saw them through Jennifer's eyes as if they were the remnants of an earlier life. The room I had lived in since I was a child was no longer familiar to me. The opera was still playing but I didn't recognize who was singing.

"Do you have a boyfriend now?" I asked, trying not to sound like a fool.

"I've been with lots of guys," she said. "The first time was with one of my father's friends. My father would kill him if he ever found out."

I was sure that at any moment she was going to get up and leave. She would make some excuse, a forgotten appointment, she could say anything. She would struggle into her boots, button her coat, kiss me on the cheek and leave. There was no way I could hold her here if she didn't want to stay. I couldn't understand why she wanted to stay, given my lack of experience.

She knelt on the floor at the foot of my bed and began fumbling with my belt. She unlaced my shoes and lowered my pants over my knees.

"You're a virgin, aren't you," she said. It wasn't a question but simply a statement for which she knew the answer. "Most of the guys I know go to a prostitute for the first time." She touched my cock with the tip of her tongue. It was something the woman from the opera house did in my fantasy. I put my hands on the top of her head, my heart beating too fast to speak. I was worried that I was going to come in her mouth.

"There are a lot of girls who charge money to do this," she said. "But I'm going to do it for free."

After a few minutes she stood up, unfastened her skirt and took off her tights.

"It must be strange to share a room with your sister," she said, glancing at the wall of photographs as if she was seeing them for the first time.

Her hands were cold. I thought of the woman at the opera, how she had leaned against me in the dark, the sleeve of my jacket brushing against the sleeve of her dress. Jennifer stretched out on my bed like a cat and pulled me down on top of her. The bones of her necklace scratched against my chest. She spread her legs, reached between our bodies and put my cock inside her. I knew I was supposed to move but I wasn't sure how. I couldn't understand how the weight of my body, pressed flat against her, wasn't causing her pain.

I thought of the shoebox filled with money in the depths of the closet. My sister said she knew where our parents kept the rest of the money, but she wouldn't tell me. I thought of Harris and what he would say when I told him I was no longer a virgin, of the singer who played Isolde lifting her arms towards heaven, of the woman in high heels sitting beside me at the opera, of my mother weeping at the kitchen table, of my father drinking soup through a straw. I saw my sister Liddy running into the bathroom to get dressed so I wouldn't see her naked. When we were children it never bothered her whether I saw her naked or not, but now she had to close a door between us whenever she wanted to get dressed. All the images of everyone I knew faded away and there was only Jennifer's eyes staring up at me.

The great melody that encompassed Isolde's final song pulsed in the air around us. Jennifer twisted her head from side to side as I moved inside her, laughing and crying at the same time. My pants were tangled around my ankles but I didn't want to stop to take them off. She had pulled up her turtleneck so that her breasts pressed against my bare chest.

"It's so beautiful," she repeated. The music, the snow, our bodies — I assume she meant everything. I felt a kind of desultory happiness, like I was floating on the surface of a lake covered with weeds. The music was subsiding, growing fainter, but Isolde's voice echoed in the distance as if she was calling my name.

I slipped out, breathing heavily, and rolled onto my side on the narrow bed.

Jennifer, still on her back, touched the wetness between her legs, put her fingers in her mouth and sucked them dry.

"All your stuff is coming out of me," she said, pulling up her tights.

THE ACTING LESSON

The movie opens with a shot of a middle-aged man in steel-rimmed glasses emerging from the back of a taxi in midtown Manhattan. As the credits roll, he enters an office building, nods hello to the security guard in the lobby, and takes his place in front of the express elevator: first stop twentieth floor. The camera adjusts to the lines of his face as they merge with the intricate shadings of marble and chrome. There are other people in the elevator, strangers who work on different floors and who know one another by sight, and the camera observes them as well: alert to the silence, the boredom, the resignation, the inevitable bitterness that surfaces when you work at a job you hate. As he steps out of the elevator, the camera pans to the end of a long corridor where a young woman is staring transfixed at the name on the door of an office. It's not clear whether she emerged from a staircase or from another elevator. There's a close-up of her face, how she lowers her eyes when she sees the man walking towards her. There's a shot of her blue high heel open-toe shoes, the way the light from the window behind her frames her hair like a golden tiara. With every step forward the distance between them decreases: we see the woman from the man's point of view as a vague outline which slowly evolves like a Polaroid into a whole person with recognizable features. There's a quick shot as the woman lifts her hand to brush a strand of blonde hair from in front of her eyes, a nervous gesture, or stares down at the black and white tiled floor of the corridor. There's a shot of the man's face as he undresses her in his mind. Though in some situations mouthing "hello" or "good morning" to a stranger is an appropriate response, the woman doesn't want to send a message that might be interpreted as a sign of interest. As they draw closer, it becomes increasingly difficult for the man to avert his eyes, while the woman edges closer to the wall of the corridor, bumping against it like a blind person. "If he touches me," she thinks, playing out the worst possible scenario, "I'll scream."

Equidistant from the points at which you and the woman first begin approaching one another, there's an office with a doctor's name stenciled on the door. It's your name, and the woman is your first appointment of the day. In a minute you'll see her naked body under a white open-backed gown on a table, her platinum blonde hair hanging over the edge. You'll hammer at her knee to check her reflexes but she won't even flinch. You'll pretend that your thoughts are organized into fleeting units of desire which you can instruct the way a sign on a road signals a car forward, or simply to yield. The dialogue in your head (between you and yourself, between her and you) consists of words of anticipation, reassurance and pleasure. You keep her at a distance, tempting fate, as she turns on her side, adjusting the gown over her shoulders and breasts. The brain might burst under the weight of a million sentence fragments, the actual words you attribute to the parts of her body or your emotions, but you don't say anything for fear she'll slam the door and leave, or sue you for taking advantage of her in the privacy of your office. In a space behind a curtain in a corner where no one can see her, she lifts her dress over her head in a comedy of errors which spells out the ambivalence of desire. What was once an abstract idea of a body under a short, sleeveless pastel dress, is arranged in front of you on a table, an *object d'art* for your pleasure alone. As you press the end of the stethoscope against her bare skin you can hear the sound of her heels (as you heard them a few moments before) on the tiles of the corridor, echoing to you out of the recent past, the gray and blue light from the windows at either end framing her waist-length blonde hair like an aura, an angelic halo. But the person who turned away in fear when she saw you coming isn't the same person whose body you're scrutinizing now. "How long have you been feeling this way?" you ask, in your most professional manner, and without hesitating she responds: "All my life, doctor. All my life."

The actor's day begins the moment he awakens. It's possible to say that he's never not acting, never unaware that he's playing a role. He pretends that he's at a table in a restaurant and that he's addressing a waiter who hovers over him and points out the day's specials on the menu. The scene in the play for which he's auditioning involves talking to a waiter in a crowded restaurant. He acts out the scene, improvising his own gestures, remembering what it feels like to eat alone, all the times he's dined alone in the evening after working in an office all day. He pretends to drink from an invisible cup of coffee which the waiter has just brought him. He bends his fingers into the ear of the handle and lifts the cup to his lips. Then he replaces it on the saucer, careful not to spill. It's his job, as an actor, to convince the audience that he's drinking from a real cup of coffee. He runs his tongue over his chapped lips to convey a sense of pleasure at the taste of the coffee. A woman he knew as a child, a friend of his mother's, appears at the door of the restaurant, her stringy brown hair hanging straight down over the frayed colors of her fur-lined coat. He pretends not to notice her (he wishes he had brought a book with him so he could bury his head) but she recognizes him at once. He stands up to meet her embrace (a kiss on either cheek) and watches as she drapes her coat over the back of a chair. She doesn't ask permission to sit at the table nor inquire whether he's expecting anyone to join him. The actor rehearses the scene, alone in his apartment. He tries to communicate to the imaginary audience a sense of annoyance at the woman for distracting him, but she's too self-involved to notice. (The audience sees every-thing; the woman sees only herself.) It's just a matter of time before she's confiding her most intimate secrets: that she's been married for five years ("to a doctor") but that she's unable to have his chil-dren. "Any" children is more accurate, but by saying "his" she puts part of the blame on her husband, inaccurately implying that she might be able to have children with someone else. She's the type of person who confides her secrets to anyone, who talks without listening, a rush of sentence fragments with no boundaries. The actor, playing the role of a young man, shakes his head as if to deny what she says is true. He's secretly worried that he looks too old for the part, that no one will believe this woman is twice his age. He attempts to convey to the woman that he understands the extent of her unhappiness but there's nothing in his own experi-ence to compare with her inability to have a child. There's no way he can imagine what it feels like to be her.

The actor sits at a table in the center of the stage, pretending to drink from a cup of coffee. He wants to give the members of the acting class the impression that the coffee is too hot to drink. There are twenty students in the class, not counting the teacher, who is also the director of the play, and who stands behind the students in the back row of the small theater. The actor tilts the imaginary cup to his lips and winces as he swallows the hot coffee. Then he returns the cup to the saucer without spilling it. He uses both hands, focusing all his attention on the empty space between his fingers. A second actor, playing the role of the waiter, approaches the table and offers him a menu. The actor listens attentively as the waiter recites the day's specials: braised duck in red wine sauce with mashed potatoes, grilled salmon, a Black Angus steak in sauce Béarnaise. Then he opens the menu, which is the size of a large magazine, and begins studying the lists of appetizers and desserts. He pushes the imaginary cup and saucer to one side to make room for the menu. In a few minutes the waiter will return, but the actor isn't ready to order.

Where does the coffee go when it passes between the lips? He feels the warmth of the liquid through the handle of the cup. It's his job, as an actor, to express the sensation he's feeling in his fingers as he lifts the cup to his lips. If the cup is full, won't he need more than one finger to lift it? The last thing he wants is to spill coffee on his shirt. He tries to take into account the smell of the coffee (smell and taste are different pleasures) and he does this by closing his eyes in a kind of ecstasy as he takes the first sip. In this gesture, the pleasure of taste and smell are combined. He puts one hand under the imaginary cup to prevent it from spilling. It's at this point that the waiter approaches the table with a large cardboard menu. But first he introduces himself: "My name is Alex," he says. "I'm your waiter."

The woman patient says "I like it when you touch me." The doctor, either absentmindedly or purposefully, has neglected to put on his latex gloves when he examines her. She's lying on a table in his office, her white gown untied, her legs raised slightly, her long platinum blonde hair hanging like a waterfall over the edge. A still life of a waterfall. Her eyes are closed. The doctor places his hand over her heart and for a moment her whole body grows tense, then relaxes, as he massages her shoulders, then tenses again, as he touches her breasts. More than once, when she was younger, a teacher in school tried to molest her. "You have a beautiful body," the doctor is tempted to say. He pushes her hair away from her ears and massages her neck with both hands. It's then that the woman tells him how much she likes it when he touches her. He translates her words into an invitation, then rejects it. For emphasis, she relaxes her legs on the end of the table, parting them slightly so that the gown slips away.

He can hear the sound of her heels as she approaches him from the end of the corridor. (Already, even before he sees her close up, he can imagine her naked body on the table in his office.) She's wearing a dress with a short skirt and stockings, a heavy gold belt, a velvet jacket with wide collars. The corridor is lined with doors, heavy fake wooden doors, leading to the offices of doctors and dentists and lawyers. When he first sees her, he has no way of knowing that she's coming to visit him. It's five minutes to nine, a Thursday morning, she's his first appointment of the day. Apparently, she just stepped off the elevator a few minutes before him and is reading the names on all the doors of the offices. At least that's what she's pretending to do when he sees her walking towards him from the other end. It's no accident, then, that they meet in front of the office with his name. "Are you here to see Dr. Inrati?" she asks. "I am Dr. Inrati," he says. His hands tremble as he turns the knob.

One wall of the office is covered with framed diplomas from universities and medical associations. You can buy them anywhere: who can tell whether they're authentic or fake? On another wall a cluster of photographs, typical of many doctor's offices, black and white photos of Venice, the roofs of Florence. A couple (doctor and wife?) stepping into a gondola. The same couple at a table in an outdoor café. The woman enters the office without seeing any of it. She sees everything but translates it all into a single impression: no details, no identification of objects, no names, just a sense of the way everything fits. Is this place threatening or not? Ever since the accident, or so she refers to it in her head, voice one talking to voice two, she assesses every situation as threatening, possibly threatening, or safe. All her actions are determined by this gauge which is active twenty-four hours. Sometimes the messages she gives herself contradict her voices; sometimes, when the gauge reads "threatening," she doesn't flinch or turn away. There's often a pleasure in the possibility of experiencing something potentially dangerous or frightening. You lose a sense of where one thought starts and another begins. You wake at noon and don't know the name of the person sleeping beside you. Fear is seductive if it talks to you sweet. What's shocking to the woman as she enters the doctor's office is the emptiness of it all. No fear, but something unnamable, worse than fear, ghostlike, the pretense of living. She had felt it on the first visit, this twinge, her third or seventh sense warning her that emptiness (the absence of feeling) is worse than fear. Or could be. Those diplomas in their cheap silver frames, those photographs in homage to some ridiculous moment of illusory happiness, all communicate one thing: the person who works in this room doesn't know what it means to be alive. One way of dealing with fear is to be aware of the possibility: to court it, let it swallow you whole, while staying outside yourself. The only way to survive is to cheat a little, seeing yourself from a distance, from the sky, until you no longer know your own body. "You can go in now, Ms. Hendrix," the receptionist says, pointing towards the hallway leading to his office. She stands behind the partition and strips, ties the gown behind her back. This is her second visit, she knows the ritual. "And how do you feel today?" the doctor asks as he enters the office, clipboard in hand. Empty, like you, she feels tempted to say. She's lying on the table, her long bleached blonde hair hanging over the edge, staring up at the ceiling, aware of every movement, the pen slipping from his hand and striking the metal bridge of the clipboard, the way he clears his throat to fill the silence, the strip of plaster dangling from the ceiling (not only isn't he alive, but this person going through the motions isn't even aware of his surroundings, can't even see), the music *easy listening* from another office. "Any better today?" he says, the machine says, forgetting that he already asked, unnerved by her beauty, the way her body fills the whole table, the largesse of her presence. It's been so long since he felt anything about anyone he doesn't even recognize what's happening to him. Two phrases, *reflecting emptiness* and *being alive*, contest one another in the air, in his head. All he knows is that he wants to cross the room, remove the photographs from their hooks on the wall, and smash them to the floor. His hands tremble as he massages her neck and he backs away, takes off his glasses and wipes them on the sleeve of his jacket. The woman lowers the gown to her waist and raises her body on one elbow. "Is there anything wrong?"

It's late afternoon, not quite dinner hour, and there are more waiters than customers in the restaurant. All the waiters are dressed alike: loose black pants, red cummerbunds, white shirts (no ties). When the woman enters, they surround her like suitors at a party vying for her attention, but she doesn't even see them. Her gaze is fixed on the young man sitting in the corner, the young out-of-work actor (the actor playing the role of actor), who has barely enough money to buy himself a decent meal. The waiter named Alex who brought the actor his coffee and took his order assumed he was dining alone. The woman scrapes the chair back, drapes her coat, flattens ankle-length woolen skirt over thighs. If there were a full-length mirror nearby she would inspect herself carefully before sitting down. But the only mirror is in the eyes of the young actor eating his imaginary dinner. The woman, the doctor's wife, played by another actress also hoping for a role in the play, another member of the acting class, settles into the chair, leans her elbows on the table. "And what have you been doing all this time?" she asks the actor. Only the night before, actor and actress rehearsed this scene together, pretending that the kitchen table in the actor's apartment was the table in the restaurant. After several hours, the actress, in her mid-thirties, the mother of a teenage son, suggested that they go to bed together. She assumed that their range of emotions as actor and actress would be enhanced if they got to know each other more intimately. People who get up on a stage night after night have to do something to keep their performances from going stale. Besides, it was too late to take the subway home and the woman didn't want to spend the money on a taxi. She took the actor's hand and placed it down the front of her blouse, but he pushed her away. It was then that he confessed to her that he wasn't interested in sleeping with women.

An orchestral version of "Greensleeves" was playing over a hidden speaker in a corner of the doctor's office. The woman lay on her stomach on the table while the doctor massaged her shoulders and back. Instead of saying "How do you feel today?" he had merely smiled at her when she stepped from behind the screen in her white gown. This was her third visit, but she felt like she had known the touch of his hands for years. She had knotted her hair into a braid so it wouldn't get in the way. "I like your hair loose," the doctor said. "It makes you look younger." She reminded herself to wear it down for her next visit. She told him how all the boys in high school used to make fun of her because of the size of her breasts. She felt the weight of her breasts against the white napkin that covered the length of the table. An oval of morning sunlight expands across the wall, reflecting the glass in which the doctor's diplomas are encased. He was tempted to tell her about his wife, how they were trying to have a child, how she had begun taking drugs to make her more fertile but without any success. After the visit, the woman stands very close to him as she buttons her blouse. There's no reason, at least in her mind, to feel self-conscious about dressing or undressing in his presence. She sits on the edge of the table, legs crossed, brushing her hair, while the doctor writes mean-ingless numbers on her chart, pretending she isn't there.

Sometimes, to amuse him, she would enter her bedroom in a white gown similar to the one she wore in his office. They would pretend he was "the doctor" and she was "the patient" (since by now she considered herself "cured" of whatever had been wrong with her), only instead of the hard table in his office she was lying on her stomach across her bed, and he was leaning over her, massaging her neck and shoulders ("How are you feeling today?"), while with his free hand he would unzip his pants and hover between her legs. By then, he had told her more than once how his marriage was falling apart over the issue of having a baby, that when he was home he felt he was playing the role of "dutiful husband," that when he made love to his wife he pretended he was making love to her. As he drove home from her apartment after midnight he rehearsed what he would tell his wife if she asked him where he had been. That they could no longer live together, that it was insane to continue this endless role-playing, that he had fallen in love with someone else, that his new lover (his former patient) was pregnant with his child. His wife never questioned why he was coming home so late, night after night. She assumed he was sleeping with someone else (this wasn't the first time he had been unfaithful to her) but it was beneath her dignity to act jealous, to play the role of the jealous wife. She sat in bed reading until she heard his key in the front door; then she turned out the bedside lamp and pretended to be asleep.

The doctor's wife told the out-of-work actor what had happened to her the last time she was in this restaurant, maybe ten years before. They were lifting imaginary forks and spoons to their mouths, going through the motions of carving and chewing (in the actual play, of course, there would be real food on real plates), gesticulating with their hands and faces to simulate the pleasures of eating. "It was before I was married," the doctor's wife said. "I would often eat out alone. The restaurant was more crowded than it is tonight. I was sitting at a table in a corner" — she gestured with her fork — "when four men came in with ski masks over their faces and guns in their hands. Almost every table in the restaurant was taken. People were eating, laughing, talking. Music was playing in the background, recorded music, the kind they play in elevators. The four gunmen ordered all the men to empty their pockets into a black garbage sack. One of the gunmen herded the waiters and the cook into the kitchen. The men in the restaurant were forced to undress, while another one of the gunmen went around and gathered all the jewelry from the women. One of the men refused and the gunman who seemed to be the leader shot him in the side of the head. There was one young woman who seemed paralyzed by what was happening; she sat at a table crying and refused to give up her ring. The head gunman tied her hands behind her back with wire, taped her mouth, pulled up her dress and raped her on the floor of the restaurant in full sight of everyone else. I gave them everything they wanted, of course. When the rape was going on there wasn't a sound except for the young woman's muffled cries; and then the cry of pleasure as the gunman with the ski mask collapsed on top of her. The three other gunmen looked envious of their leader. For a moment it seemed that each of them was going to take his turn with the young woman on the floor. There was a pool of blood surrounding the body of the man they had shot and I guess they figured they had wasted enough time torturing us. They backed out of the restaurant with their guns raised, carrying the sack of money and jewelry, and disappeared into the night. The police arrived, in due time, and questioned everyone who was there. The man who had been shot was dead; I don't know what happened to the young woman. I had to go down to the police station and answer questions for hours." Her food was getting cold as she told the story. The young actor, his fork raised, stared at her in disbelief. "You mean it all happened here? In this restaurant?" "Right here," the woman said, pointing to a spot on the carpet. "That's where he raped her."

"More than once," the woman says, "when I was younger, a teacher tried to molest me." They're lying across her bed, both fully dressed, a bottle of cognac and two wineglasses on a tray between them. The doctor is too exhausted to pay attention to yet another chapter of her life story; in his fantasy, he had imagined arriving in her apartment, making love on the living room floor, and leaving. For weeks now she's been trying to convince him to spend the night with her. It's been years since she slept with anyone, since she woke up in the morning with another body lying beside her. The doctor is thinking about his wife, what her life will be like after they separate. He feels like taping the woman's mouth, shackling her wrists, and forcing her to do whatever he wants. But when he actually suggests making love in this manner, simulating the rape scene which took place when she was nineteen, she shakes her head sadly. "You're missing the point," she says. The doctor has the impression that they'll never get past this moment, never move forward into a present tense free from the shadows of the past. His wife, the rape scene, the way the teachers used to go out of their way to touch her arms and shoulders and breasts, casually, as if they were just being affectionate, as if they weren't aware of what they were doing: all associations related to the stigmas of the past will linger forever. All these wounds feel like they were inflicted yesterday. He tries to convey to the audience his frustration without losing their sympathy, but the point of view has changed from the doctor to his former patient. He reaches out and touches her shoulders and begins to unbutton her blouse as she talks, but she pushes his hand away. "I won't fuck you again," she says, loud and clear, "until you leave your wife."

The waiting room of the doctor's office is filled with young women. Some of them are reading magazines, others stare into space. None of them are happy, the woman thinks, not certain whether she's projecting her own feelings or whether what her instinct tells her is true. Since she met the doctor, she no longer thinks of her life as "happy" or "miserable." There's no longer a fixed boundary between one emotion or another. The receptionist calls out her name, "Ms. Hendrix," and the doctor's assistant leads the patient behind the screen. "You can undress here," she says, "the doctor will be with you in a minute." The patient lifts her dress over her head, reaches behind her back to unfasten her bra. She remembers the way her first boyfriend, when she was in high school, used to fumble at the catch of her bra while she pretended she wasn't aware of his difficulties. Finally he gave up (she felt like laughing in his face), lowered the straps of her bra over her arms, and buried his face between her breasts. She stares at the gown hanging from a hook on the wall and decides not to wear it. By the time the doctor enters the office, clipboard in hand, the young woman is lying naked with her knees raised on the silver table.

Lying in bed waiting for him to appear, each night a little later and with a different excuse, the doctor's wife reviewed their life together as a series of glyphs which translated into a small gallery of memories with no continuity and no emotion. The person she had married six years ago in a ceremony in a church was more alive in memory than this absent lover, but even that spark was going out. The fire was out, there were only dead embers, wet kindling, who cared if he came back or not? She wanted to tell the young man whom she had met earlier that evening in the restaurant how her husband slept with other women (as if no one had ever been unfaithful before) but she was frightened that he would hate her for breaking down in public, that her tears would embarrass him, that he wouldn't know how to react. Even telling him that she wasn't able to have babies had been a mistake. She had to admit that meeting him had distracted her in a positive way from her problems with her husband. One day, she told herself, when he returned home late, she wouldn't be there. She laughed out loud as she imagined him standing over the empty bed. She pictured herself with her own lover, the young actor she had met that day, his tiny one room walk-up, the loft bed, the alcove which served as a kitchen. She had to remind herself that she was only thirty-five, still young enough to change her life, that it wasn't unusual for women her age to have lovers who were ten years younger. Most days she lacked the strength to lift her head from the pillow. Most days she didn't even bother getting dressed. Before leaving the restaurant, she and the young actor exchanged phone numbers and he told her she could call him any time. The idea that he might be waiting for her phone call right at that moment, though it was two in the morning, was enough to get her out of bed and search through the pockets of her coat for the old matchbook on which she had written his number. She could see him lying in bed, wide awake, fully dressed, smoking, listening with anticipation to the sound of the phone. "Answer it, you bastard," the woman said. But as soon as she heard his voice — it seemed to be coming from a thousand miles away, lost in space — she hung up.

I used to meet people in parks or bars, the young woman told the doctor, and take them home with me. The only men who interested me were men I'd never met before and would never see again. I haunted deserted playgrounds late at night and if I saw a young man on a bench I would make eye contact and approach him. The only men who interested me were men I didn't know. Sometimes I would meet someone at a party and make love in a deserted bedroom with the lights off so I couldn't see his face. Once, in a taxi late at night with the driver, a Palestinian who had the word "Allah" tattooed in a heart on his arm. We made eye contact in the rearview mirror, I unbuttoned my blouse. The only men I was attracted to were strangers, men with no names. I would arrive at parties in a short skirt with no underwear and sit in a corner until someone approached me. I liked to make love to two or three men at one time. Some of this is true, some of these are my fantasies. If they wanted, I let them tie my hands behind my back with a nylon stocking or a scarf and tape my mouth so I couldn't cry out. Afterwards, I would lie on my stomach while they got dressed, not moving until I heard the door slam behind them. That was my dream, anyway, but it never worked out. The first time, with you, in the office, I can't tell you how much I wanted you to touch me. I didn't want to get dressed. I felt it the first time I saw you, in the corridor, coming towards me. Whether we made love or not, I knew I'd come back for more.

I was only nineteen. We were going to be married that fall. My fiancé had given me an engagement ring and we went out to a restaurant with members of his family to celebrate. We were just finishing our dinners, my fiancé was drinking coffee, I was sipping

Chevas Regal, when four men with ski masks pulled tight over their faces entered the restaurant. Each of them was carrying a gun. My fiancé, his father and brother were forced to undress, along with the other men in the restaurant. They were led into a room in the back, the freezer, while one of the men went from table to table gathering the jewelry from the women. I refused to give him my ring. He pulled me by the hair and dragged me to a space between tables in the center of the restaurant. He tied my hands behind my back and taped my mouth. I have to confess that I wasn't a virgin. My fiancé and I had been sleeping together for over a year and I'd had other boyfriends before that. Don't ask me how many. The man with the gun rolled me over onto my stomach and forced me to spread my legs. I don't know how long it lasted: maybe five or six minutes. They had already shot one of the men in the restaurant and I was frightened that they would kill me as well if I refused. At some point I stopped struggling; I felt like I was going to faint. I kept going to the verge of blacking out and then snapping back. There was a voice in my head reminding me that it wasn't a dream, no nightmare, but really happening. I can still feel his hands in my hair, the smell of his breath on the back of my neck. When it was over he pulled off my ring and put it in his pocket. He stood up, buttoned his pants, and kicked me with the toe of his boot. I could hear his friends laughing in the background. 'It's my turn now,' one of them said, but he never did anything. I kept lying on the floor of the restaurant waiting for one of the other men to climb on top of me. Of course, the wedding was called off. I refused to even see my fiancé. He would call me every day for months after but I refused to speak with anyone, especially him. I dropped out of college and hid myself in my bedroom in my parents' house. There was my photograph in the newspaper, the girl who was raped in the restaurant. Some days I didn't even get out of bed. I would come downstairs to eat and watch television with my family but my father always ended up carrying me upstairs. The police questioned me over and over again, but they never found the men. They assumed because I was raped by one of them that I knew something no one else did. Apparently one of the customers in the restaurant was a state senator so the story received more publicity than it might have otherwise. One of the detectives who was assigned to the case kept calling me long after the publicity had stopped. I realized that he wasn't just calling me because of what had happened in the restaurant but that he was falling in love with me. He would call the house to assure my family that the case hadn't been forgotten, that he was still working on it. But after awhile I told my parents to say I wasn't home, that I was busy, that I had moved away. Part of me, I know, didn't want him to find the man who had raped me. I wanted the event to recede, as doctors assured me it would: I wanted to get on with my life. I even knew that I could deny it had ever happened if I wanted to. I was good at denying, good at lying to myself, good at pretense. Just when I thought I was almost cured I started falling down at unexpected moments, paralyzed, gasping for air. It was as if my body was trying to remind me that it was stronger than any attempt I was making to pretend that nothing was bothering me and the only way I could get beyond the experience was by accepting it as something that could have happened to anyone. I lingered over the moments in the restaurant like frozen stills from a grade-B movie. I wanted to think so hard about what had happened that I'd bury it forever under the weight of my obsession. I even returned to the restaurant and sat at the same table where I was sitting the night it happened. I went there more than once. I would go alone, hoping a stranger would join me. I'd stare at all the single men standing at the bar and dare them with my eyes. I was like the shell-shocked veteran of some meaningless war who has to relive her combat experiences in order to integrate them into her present reality. Most of all, I remember the way he kicked me when I was lying on the floor. I can still feel the toe of his boot against my ribs. As if I were a bag of trash. Trash! And that's what I've felt like ever since.

The play consists of four main characters: a doctor, his wife, the patient who becomes his lover, and an out-of-work actor who is also an old friend of the doctor's wife. There are other characters as well: the four gunmen who raid the restaurant, all the customers in the restaurant (including the young woman's future husband and father-in-law), the waiter, the doctor's receptionist. In the first scene we see two people walking towards one another down an empty corridor lined with doctor's offices. It takes about five seconds for the two strangers to meet, center stage, at the door of the office with the doctor's name on it. Their hands reach out simultaneously for the doorknob but the doctor gets there first. He smiles at the woman who removes her hand and holds it behind her back as if she's frightened that touching the doctor's hand will contaminate her. Subsequent scenes include the doctor's waiting room, his office, and the restaurant where the actor and the doctor's wife meet accidentally. The doctor's wife (Clarissa) tells the young unemployed actor (Bob) that ten years ago, more than that, four men with guns entered the restaurant and murdered one of the customers and raped a young woman. How the male customers were forced to strip naked and were herded into the freezer and how the women were forced to turn over all their jewelry. Unlike Greek drama, the murder and the rape take place on stage, in full view of the other customers in the restaurant and the audience. There's another character I've forgotten about: the detective who falls in love with the woman who was raped. Neither the playwright nor the director are sure how old the detective should be. The director insists that all the actors and actresses are chosen from his acting class. The playwright wants a well known actor and actress to play the parts of the doctor and his lover. For a week, playwright and director don't speak to one another. There's a rumor that the play will be canceled or that the playwright is going to find another director. All the students in the class are aware that this power struggle is going on. Each of them takes a turn on the stage playing the roles of the doctor, the patient, the doctor's wife, or the young actor in the restaurant. Everyone has a different theory how the rape scene should be treated. One student, a male, feels that the young woman and the rapist should really do it, really fuck, really make love, every performance. Others think it should happen off stage or behind a screen while still others think the actors could simulate the rape like they do in the movies. One of the students, a young actress named Natalie, confesses to the class that she was raped when she was nineteen, in circumstances similar to those in the play. The last thing she wants is to relive this experience night after night. Yet the fact that she knows what it feels like is also a point in her favor.

The director lies in bed and imagines a possible movie version of the play. The credits roll over a shot of the doctor entering the office building where he works, riding the elevator, stepping out and seeing the woman at the end of a long corridor. There's a close-up of the woman's face, how she lowers her eyes when she sees the man walking towards her. There's a shot of her blue high heel shoes, the way the light from the window behind her frames her hair like a golden tiara. The doctor turns over on his side and touches the face of the woman named Natalie who's sleeping beside him, the actress who's going to play the role of the young woman in the play. "You're not giving me the part because I'm sleeping with you?" she had asked him earlier, knowing the answer in advance, but wondering whether he had the nerve to tell her the truth. There's no reason why she would dream of sleeping with him if he wasn't the director of the play. She had been abused enough by men in her short life. She knew how to lie back and spread her legs and endure it, close her eyes, until it was over. There was no question in the director's mind that she was perfect for the role. He reminded her, as he did all the actors and actresses in the class, about Stanislavski's theory of "emotion memory," how you relive your emotions about an event in the past in order to communicate a similar emotion to the audience. So that it was up to Natalie, when she was being raped on stage, to remember how she felt when she had really been raped, no matter how painful the memory. The more she remembered, the better her performance would be. The director forces her to explore every detail, every nuance of feeling surrounding the event. "He wants me to tell him that I enjoyed it," she says to herself. "But it isn't true."

OTHER TRIP STREET PRESS BOOKS

2000andWhat?   A collection of 20 short stories about the turn of the millennium featuring both known and emerging writers of innovative fiction. What unifies these writers is their ability to avoid a predictable response to an inevitable event. Stories by Etel Adnan, Margaret Atwood, Frederick Barthelme, Lydia Davis, David Gilbert, Steve Katz, Kevin Killian, Donna Levreault, Harry Mathews, Ameena Meer, Susan Smith Nash, Niels Nielsen, Karl Roeseler, Teri Roney, Linda Rudolph, Kevin Sampsell, Lynne Tillman, Karen Tei Yamashita, Lewis Warsh and Mac Wellman.

ISBN: 0963919229 $12.00

Five Happiness by David Gilbert.   A 92-page puzzle of wit and audacious poetic technique. The narrative is a dance of characters that appear and disappear without warning. Fiction has never been so strange. "Captivating brilliant prose that may be blinding to the normal eye." — *Kevin Sampsell*

ISBN: 0963919202 $6.95

The Adventures of Gesso Martin by Karl Roeseler.   "Karl Roeseler takes a straightforward situation — a wandering rock star, a lion, seven French maids — and, with good humor and a charming light touch, rings magical changes on it. Particle by particle, with glittering clarity, the world of the fortunate Gesso Martin, the gentle chauffeur-cum-philosopher, gradually accumulates around us in an engagingly fantastic tale..." — *Lydia Davis*

ISBN: 0963919210 $8.95

Doomsday Belly by Susan Smith Nash.   A collection of longer stories from the author of *Channel-Surfing the Apocalypse*. Susan Smith Nash possesses the rare ability to write about topical events and issues without being predictable or mundane. Oklahoma will never be the same. "Susan Smith Nash is a reporter commissioned by the Muses... reporting live from all the intimate and mysterious combat zones that fill our world with terror." — *Robert Kelly*

(Forthcoming in 1997)

Order directly from our distributor, Small Press Distribution (1-800-869-7553), from amazon.com or from your favorite bookstore.

Trip Street Press is dedicated to the notion that a book publisher's identity only emerges through the juxtaposition of the books it publishes.